Y FIC LUC
Lucido, Aimee
Recipe for disaster

Recipe FOR Disaster

Recipe FOR Disaster

by Aimee Lucido

Versify
Houghton Mifflin Harcourt
Boston   New York

Versify® is an imprint of Houghton Mifflin Harcourt Publishing Company. Versify is a registered trademark of Houghton Mifflin Harcourt Publishing Company.

hmhbooks.com

The text was set in Scala.

Hand-lettering by Emma Trithart

Cover and interior design by Celeste Knudsen

The Library of Congress Cataloging-in-Publication Data is on file.

ISBN: 978-0-358-38691-9

Manufactured in the United States of America

1 2021

4500830924

For Ma and Pop,
who gave me permission

Recipe for My Family

Mix together
one (1) Mom
    named Liat
    with big curly hair
    she always wears straight
    who works as a biology professor
    at the university across from my school
and one (1) Dad
    named Richard
    with a bald patch
    and a gap between his front teeth
    who works as a financial . . .
    . . . something-or-other.
Bake in Chicago for six years
    at -10 degrees in the winter
    and 110 degrees in the summer
and add one (1) baby boy
    named Samuel
    and love him
    like he's never going to grow up.
Bake for five more years
and add one (1) baby girl

named Hannah
and raise her to be . . .
. . . well, me, I guess.
Bake for five more years
before adding one (1) Grandma Mimi
(my mom's mom)
who will put a whisk in Sam's hand
and a spatula in mine
and it will feel like they've been there
all along.

Bake for seven more years
but be careful
because a happy family
is more delicate than a cheese soufflé:
perfectly balanced
until it's not.

Then, beware
the
f
a
l
l

Fall

Fall

Fall is when we make rugelach.

"In honor of Shira's bat mitzvah!" Grandma Mimi says today.

I lift my spatula in agreement and call out "Hear, hear!" while Sam does the same with his whisk.

My family will take any excuse to bake rugelach. It makes the house smell like fall—butter and chocolate with a hint of cinnamon—and even though no one needs an excuse, it's tradition to come up with one anyway.

Today, that excuse is my best friend's bat mitzvah.

"Hannah?" Dad walks into the kitchen half dressed, waving a folded piece of paper. "Mom wants you to write Shira a note in her card before we all sign . . . ooh, chocolate!" He reaches into the bowl of rugelach filling, card forgotten, and—Slap!

"Ow! Miriam!" Dad licks the chocolate from his fingers. "I wanted to taste your *arugula!*"

Grandma Mimi whisks the bowl of filling off the countertop and points a floury finger toward the door. "On rugelach day, the kitchen is a Jewish space." She says it all stern, but her eyes are laughing as she talks.

Dad waves his sticky hand at me and Sam. "Then what are they doing in here? They're not really Jewish!"

"Rude!" calls Sam, and I laugh.

"My grandchildren?" says Grandma Mimi, tugging at her Star of David necklace. "My Hannah? My Sam? With me as their grandmother, they're as Jewish as they come! Besides, have you seen how they roll rugelach?"

"Yeah, Dad!" I beam at Grandma Mimi and point to my perfectly crafted rugelach crescent. "We're as Jewish as they come!"

Dad laughs and tries again to reach into the bowl of chocolate filling, but Grandma Mimi pulls it away. "Richard, you're going to make us late. And you, Hannah?" She turns to me. "Go write a note to your friend. Move!"

Dad goes upstairs to get dressed, and I find a handful of colored pencils in the junk drawer.

I write:

Recipe for a She-ra

Mix together:
my #1 sous-chef
the nicest person I know
the Marlin to my Dory

the REAL winner of the sixth-grade Olympics
    (no matter what Mr. Pierri says)
Zendaya
    (just cuz)
my favorite dance partner
    the sister I never knew I needed
and you get one She-ra
(my best friend)

                                        Love,

                      Ha-na-na-na-boo-boo

P.S. You are the GOAT. And the sheep. And the cow. Moo.

P.P.S. Remember, if you get nervous, just picture Jeremy Brewer in his underwear.

Then I draw a picture of us. We're wearing the bat mitzvah dresses we bought together—caramel for her, green for me—and we're dancing to our favorite song. It's the one we chose months ago for the first partner dance of her party: "Single Ladies."

And with that, I hand the card to Sam to sign.

"When I open my own bakery," he whispers, taking the card out of my hand, "if anyone pronounces it *arugula* in my presence, I'm pressing charges."

I laugh. "You better." Then I return to Grandma Mimi's side to finish rolling rugelach, my gift to my best friend for her bat mitzvah.

Rugelach

IC butter

8 oz cream cheese

sugar to taste

salt to taste

It vanilla

2C flour

butter for brushing

Filling:

For the taste of winter use ~~cranberi~~ cranberries, apples.

In spring use berries: strawberries, blueberries . . .

Summer is ~~peach~~ peaches or plums (stone fruit)

and for fall use chocolate.

Beat butter + cream cheese + sugar + salt + vanilla

Add flour until combined.

Split dough in half and press into circles. Spread filling on
   top, cut into triangles. Roll, brush with butter, and bake
   at 375 until gold and puffy.

Remember:

Don't be greedy with the filling.

An overfull cookie leaks and burns.

Recipe for a Best Friendship

Mix together
two (2) best friends
   me
   and Shira
   who
         have seen *Finding Nemo*
         forty-one times
   who
         have built more blanket forts
         than they can remember
   who
         have spent five years
         making up recipes
         for Jeremy Brewer Brownies
         Extra Fudge Fudge Ice Cream
         and
         Snow Day Snowballs
   who
         got their braces on at the same time
         even if they won't
         get them off together
   who

have shared every secret

every story

every scheme

who

are never seen one

without the other

except Tuesdays and Thursdays

when Shira has

Hebrew school

who

once left food out for a backyard raccoon

and ended up in the hospital

for emergency rabies shots

who

have baked enough

chocolate chip cookies

and Funfetti cupcakes

and strawberry rhubarb pies

with Grandma Mimi

to feed the entire city of Chicago

for one (1) day

or two (2) best friends

for five (5)

years.

Hair

Mom comes downstairs, looking glazed and frosted, frilly and frantic. "You're not dressed, yet? We have to be at Congregation Beth Shalom in an hour! Sam, take a shower! Mom, at least wear an apron if you're going to bake in your new dress! And Hannah, shouldn't you do something with your hair?"

And okay, fine, I get it. Mom's stressing because she hates doing Jewish things.

And okay, fine, I'm sure it also has something to do with the fact that her older sister, Aunt Yael, is a rabbi at Shira's temple, and Mom hasn't seen her in, like, forever.

And okay, fine, it *does* look like Grandma Mimi has rolled around in a sack of flour.

So I get why Mom's anxious.

But did she have to take it out on my hair?

I hate my hair.

It's curly—no, frizzy—no, messy.

Always.

Doesn't matter if I brush it, wet or dry, or if I put hair gel on my comb and swipe it through.

My hair is always . . .

. . . *ugh*.

I wish I could

tame
calm
buff
shine
flatten straight
my f r i z z y
lint ball
dust bunny
cotton candy
hair,
and sometimes I wish for hair
like Shira's.

Dark brown and silky smooth, and she doesn't have to do almost anything before it shines like the mirror glaze on one of Grandma Mimi's cakes.

Maybe I should shave my head, or at least make one of Sam's baseball caps a wardrobe staple.

But today I'll settle for Mom's flat iron.

Family

Shira looks beautiful in her caramel dress. I mean, she's always beautiful, but today she's extra beautiful. Her hair is done in this braid that wraps all around her head, and the way her cousin did her makeup makes her eyes look big and soft. And in her new high heels, she's even standing differently than she usually does.

She looks my way, gives me a huge wave, and points to her teeth so I can see her braces are gone.

I give her a giant thumbs-up and smile right back.

"I'm going to say hi," says Grandma Mimi, and at first I assume she's going to say hi to Shira and her family, but Mom says, "Do what you need to do," and I realize Grandma Mimi isn't going to say hi to Shira and her family.

She's going to say hi to Aunt Yael.

Mom mutters something under her breath, and I follow Grandma Mimi with my eyes as she meets a woman I recognize immediately, even though I haven't seen her in seven years: my Aunt Yael.

They talk and laugh and squeeze each other's hands, and when Grandma Mimi gestures over to us, I see Aunt Yael's eyes flicker in our direction.

So I wave.

And why shouldn't I? Grandma Mimi clearly doesn't think she's a terrible person—she takes her out to lunch every month! And it's not like anybody has ever told me why Mom stopped talking to her seven years ago, but I guess Mom thinks I should blindly follow her lead, because as I wave to Aunt Yael, Mom pushes my hand down. "Oh, look at that, Hannah," she says in a voice all high and fake. "I found our seats!"

She grips my hand a little too tight and leads our family to our spot: RESERVED FOR THE MALFA-ADLERS.

Second row, center left.

That's right behind Shira's grandparents but in front of the rest of my class, and three different people—Dahlia Schulte, Jafari Williams, and Jeremy Brewer (who looks extra cute in one of those little round hats they have at the front of the temple)—all ask, "Why do you get to sit up there?"

I smooth out my newly straightened hair and say, "Because I'm basically family."

Hebrew

The first part of Shira's bat mitzvah is the ceremony. It's the part she refers to as "kinda boring and *really* scary." Boring because it's two hours long and mostly in Hebrew, and scary because she's leading the whole thing on a stage in front of pretty much everybody she knows. But if she can get through it all without passing out from stage fright, that's when we get to the fun part: her party.

Shira and her rabbi walk up to the podium, and the room grows quiet. Now that she's standing right in front of me, I can tell Shira's nervous. Her hands are shaking, and she keeps rocking back and forth on her new high heels while she chews all the lipstick off her bottom lip. So when she looks my way, I catch her eye. I stick out my tongue and give myself a double chin, screwing my mouth up into a cartoon frown, and that makes her laugh.

"You've got this!" I mouth to her, and by the time she's at the podium, telling everybody to turn to page 283 in our prayer books, she's smiling and her hands aren't shaking at all.

Go, Shira!

I turn to page 283, remembering just in time that the pages count backwards, and I spend fifteen minutes following along with what Shira is chanting. Then I accidentally turn two pages instead of one, and before I know it, I'm completely lost.

"What page are we on?" I whisper to Sam. But he shrugs. He's reading some poem on page 154, and I'm almost positive we never went backwards in the reading.

Or . . . would that be forward?

Anyway, I try one last time to figure out where we are, but then I close the prayer book and resign myself to listening for the remainder of the . . .

. . . one-hour-and-forty-five-minute ceremony.

Sigh.

I guess I should have expected this. I've never been able to follow along with Hebrew for more than a few minutes at a time. To be fair, I've only had a few opportunities to try. I've been inside a temple . . . what . . . three times before this?

I went once, when I was two, for a cousin's baby-naming service, once when my Grandpa Joseph died, and once for Mark Folds's bar mitzvah this past summer.

Oh, and one time, when I was eight, I begged my mom to let me go with Grandma Mimi for some big holiday. They had a fight about it, and when Mom finally agreed to let me go, I ended up falling asleep halfway through the service. So I'm not sure if that counts.

Mom never talks about Jewish stuff, and she doesn't like it when Grandma Mimi does either, so anything I do know about the Jewish side of my family, I learned through TV, social studies, and, of course, Shira.

But something weird happens once I close my prayer book. While I was trying to follow along, the words sounded like nothing I'd ever heard before, but now that my book is closed and I'm just listening the sounds of what Shira is chanting, I recognize some of it. Nothing major, just a prayer here, a song there, but it's familiar all the same. It's almost as if little bits of Hebrew have leaked into my brain over the years, like sweet syrup soaking slowly into a pound cake, and when I do recognize the music, I can't help but sing along.

Baruch atah Adonai
mmmm-mmmm-mmmm-mmmm
melech ha-o-lum
mmmm-mmmm-mmmm-mmmm
Ah —
ah —
mein!

Grandma Mimi sings as well, from the other side of the bench. She's belting out the words as loud as she can, but after a few minutes I notice that we're the only ones in our row who actually are singing.

Sam is still reading random bits of poetry he finds sprinkled through the prayer book, and Dad's checking email on his phone.

Mom also isn't singing, although something about the way she's buttoning her lips with her teeth makes me think if she opened her mouth, the words would flow out of her.

I feel silly all of a sudden. Like maybe I shouldn't be singing along at all. Like everyone is looking at me funny and whispering from behind their programs, *Wow, Hannah sure is loud. What, does she think she's Jewish or something?*

Then I feel ridiculous because I barely know every third word in these prayers. Not like Shira.

Shira. The girl who lost our middle school spelling bee in round one because she got nervous and forgot how to spell the word *different*.

The girl who last month froze in front of our English class when she had to recite a Shakespeare poem from memory.

The girl who a few minutes ago was shaking and rocking and gnawing at her lips because she was so nervous about singing in front of people.

She chants everything perfectly. She doesn't seem scared now. She doesn't stumble over words, and she has this smile on her face, like she knows she's doing a great job and is proud to be standing there.

I shouldn't be singing along at all. It's weird that I tried. So I quiet my voice and look at the bench across the room, where Aunt Yael is standing, and once I'm looking at her, I can't stop staring.

She's singing, all right. Oh boy is she singing. She's singing and rocking and smiling and hitting her hand against her thigh, and she looks so full of the song that it's bubbling out of her like water boiling in a too-small saucepan.

And as the words float around me, I find myself wishing that one day I could be like that. To know every word to every song so deeply that they take over my body. To *feel* them when I sing, as if they're a part of me, as familiar as breathing.

Dad must notice I've stopped singing, because he nudges me. "Don't you wish they'd sing in English?" he whispers. "You know, for those of us who aren't Jewish?"

He grins at me as if I'm in on the joke, but something about the way he says it bugs me.

I laugh anyway. "Heh. Yeah," I whisper back. "For those of us that aren't Jewish."

As Usual

When the ceremony is over, I practically leap out of my seat to be the first to give Shira a hug. "You did such a great job!" I say.

"Thanks." Shira shakes her head like it's no big deal. "I messed up twice," she adds.

"Oh my gosh, stop." I play-smack her on the shoulder. "No one even noticed."

Shira laughs because she knows I'm right, and I laugh because I *am* right, and we hug again, and I admire how amazing her hair looks all braided up and marvel at how straight and white her teeth are now that her braces are off, and how is it possible that Jeremy Brewer looks even cuter than usual in his hat? And do I mean a *kippah*? And yeah, I guess that is what I mean, and oh my gosh, he looks *so* cute, but isn't it weird that Kyle Goldstein brought his own kippah? And ahhhh! It's all over! I can't believe tonight is her party, and—

Someone calls Shira's name, and she turns to say hi to them. I think it's one of her Hebrew school friends.

"Bye, Shira!" I say, but she doesn't hear me.

That's okay. We'll have our big moment tonight on the dance floor. And for the time being, there's a whole line of people:

family members

neighbors

classmates

members of the temple

Jeremy Brewer

and everybody

waiting to congratulate my best friend.

Kiddush

After the service there's a mini-party, which Grandma Mimi calls a Kiddush. I fill my plate with cheese and crackers, grapes and strawberries, and a couple slices of mushy-looking apples, because everything else looks *blech*.

I hold up a dried-out piece of rugelach from the table and give Sam a look. He sticks his tongue out. "When I start my own bakery," he says, "rugelach like that will be illegal."

I laugh and go find my friends. I sit with my usual lunch crew, Delilah and Lin, Chris Rodriguez and Chris Wilcoxen, but Shira isn't with us. She's still swarmed by people wishing her "Mazel tov!"

"You tried the rugelach yet?" I ask Chris R., pointing to the rolled-up cookies on his plate.

"Rug-lah?" he asks.

"*Roog-eh-lah,*" I say slowly. "They're Jewish cookies. My grandma makes them, but these don't look very good."

"I didn't know you were Jewish," he says.

"Well, I am, but not really."

Chris R. takes a bite of rugelach but spits it out. "Blech! You're right, Hannah. Jewish food is gross!"

"Hey," I start. "That's not what I meant. My grandma makes—"

But no one wants to hear about how Grandma Mimi's rugelach tastes like fall melting on your tongue. Everyone is far more interested in discussing who they want to dance with at Shira's party tonight. Chris W. is planning to ask Blair Thornburgh, and Delilah wants Boggy to ask her, and everyone knows Chris R. is planning to ask Arjun Sawhney.

"Are you going to ask Jeremy Brewer?" Lin asks, nudging me.

I smile and shrug. "Who knows?" I say. But I do know. I'm not going to ask Jeremy Brewer, and neither is Shira. Instead of the DJ playing a slow song for the partner dance, we're going to surprise everyone with a fast one. "Single Ladies." Our best friend anthem.

Tonight, the only dance partners we need are each other.

Recipe for a Bat Mitzvah After-Party

Mix together
fifty-two (52) kids in our seventh-grade class
seventy-five (75) other guests
    family
    friends
    family friends
one (1) DJ
five (5) party facilitators
one (1) three (3)-layer cake
    covered each in sprinkles
    candy crumbles
    and coconut shavings
    from that fancy downtown bakery
    Her Cakes
six (6) sappy toasts
one (1) party dress
two (2) high-heeled shoes
one (1) brand-new
    first-ever
    iPhone
and one (1) guest of honor
    my best friend, Shira Rosen

The Best Night of Our Lives

Sometimes, when you're baking something new, you look at the recipe and have a picture in your head of what it's going to look like, smell like, taste like—and it comes out of the oven looking nothing like you pictured.

I'm seated beside Shira at dinner, but she doesn't sit down all night.

My hair shines bright and straight at first but begins to curl as I sweat.

We dance the hora in a circle, but I'm stuck holding hands with Kyle Goldstein.

We lift Shira in a chair, but I fall on my butt.

Shira has barely said two words to me since we left the temple, but when the DJ announces it's time for the first partner dance, my heart pounds. This is our moment.

All the guests gather around Shira, like we're a doughnut and she's the hole, and I stand up front so she'll see me. I wait for the opening notes of "Single Ladies," bopping my knees in anticipation, mentally rehearsing the choreography we learned four years ago during an extended summer sleepover.

But when the DJ says, "All right, bat mitzvah girl. You get

to pick a special someone to be your dance partner," it surprises everyone—

    even me—

          especially me—

               only me

when the fast-paced clapping song in my head gets
replaced by a slow, mushy piano ballad.

I try to lock eyes with Shira, to ask if maybe the DJ played
the wrong song, but Shira isn't looking at me. She's facing the
exact opposite side of the circle, walking right up to Jeremy
Brewer, and asking him to dance.

Recipe for Jeremy Brewer Brownies

Make a normal brownie batter but add . . .

   . . . extra sugar — because he's so sweet

   . . . hunks of chocolate — because

       he's a hunk (duh)

   . . . peanuts — because, to be fair, he's a

little nuts.

Firsts

Soon, everyone is dancing. One big
tangle of arms and legs. Shira
stands with Jeremy. Still.
So close together they
could smush an egg
between them, and
good thing that
Shira's braces
are now off
just in time
for her
first
kiss.

Jeremy Brewer

Nothing was ever supposed to happen with Jeremy Brewer. For either of us. Not me, and not Shira.

He was supposed to be someone to talk about at sleepovers. Someone to stare at in our yearbooks. Someone to write recipes for when we were bored and hungry. We could analyze where he sat in English class for hours—maybe he didn't sit next to you because, if he *did* sit next to you, it would look like he liked you, so he sat two seats away from you because he could actually see you better while not making it too obvious he was staring—and we could fill an entire sleepless sleepover discussing how he wore his hair.

Neither of us was supposed to dance with him tonight, and *definitely* neither of us was supposed to kiss him.

I know today is Shira's big day, and I know I'm supposed to be happy for her, and I know I'm supposed to smile and hug her and tell her it doesn't matter that she swapped out the first partner song at the last minute and it's okay that she decided to dance with Jeremy Brewer instead of me. I'm supposed to tell her how lucky he is to have kissed her, and how they make such a cute couple, and I know this, I know this, I know this.

But it's hard to make yourself feel something just because you know you're supposed to feel it.

I can't watch them anymore, so I leave the dance floor to find my family. Mom is at the bar with some of the other parents, and Dad is balancing as much cheese-and-caramel popcorn on his dessert plate as he can, and Sam is flirting with one of the dancers who looks like he's about double Sam's age. But Grandma Mimi is by herself at the table, watching everyone dance around her.

"What's wrong, bubbelah?" she asks as I sit beside her.

"Nothing," I say, but my eyes sneak back to look at Shira and Jeremy.

"Ahh," Grandma Mimi says. "I see."

"No. Don't say anything. It's not a big deal."

Grandma Mimi pats my knee. "Of course not. It's no big deal."

"It really isn't. I'm happy for her."

But these words must sound as sour as they feel, because Grandma Mimi doesn't say anything in response. Instead, she sits with me silently, watching the party spin on around us while I remake the recipe for Jeremy Brewer Brownies in my head.

The New Recipe for Jeremy Brewer Brownies

Make a normal brownie batter but ~~add~~ REMOVE . . .

. . . half the ~~extra~~ not all that sugar — because he's ~~so~~ sweet

~~. . . hunks of chocolate — because~~ UNDERBAKE it

~~he's a hunk (duh)~~ by half — because he can be SO immature

EXTRA . . . peanuts — ~~because, to be fair, he's a~~

~~little nuts.~~ BECAUSE Shira choosing Jeremy over me makes me feel like I'm going nuts.

Her Way

When the dancing stops, it's time to cut the cake. Shira floats toward me, all happy and red-faced, as if she's completely unaware that she went against our plans.

She was supposed to dance with *me* all night. Not Jeremy Brewer.

"DIDYOUSEEHIMKISSME???" she asks.

Of course I saw.

Everyone did.

"HEWANTSTOSITWITHME!"

I don't even have a chance to pretend I'm happy for her before she's being called to the front of the room to light candles, cut cake, and finally, for the first time all night, sit with me at our table.

"Shira," I whisper, poking her in the side. "What happened to 'Single Ladies' for the partner dance? We've been practicing our choreography!"

But Shira looks at me, confused. "'Single Ladies'? But the partner dance is supposed to be a slow song."

Now it's my turn to look confused. "Don't you remember? We decided months ago! You said slow dances were weird and we should surprise everyone and switch it out at the last second with something fast."

But Shira is shaking her head. "Hannah, I didn't think that was serious. I thought you knew how much I was looking forward to the partner dance."

And I'm about to tell her, yeah, I thought she was looking forward to it because it would be *our* dance, but before I have a chance to say anything, she holds a finger up. "Wait one second." She waves Jeremy Brewer over and then looks back at me with an apology face. "Actually, could you scooch down a seat?" She crinkles her nose. "Sorry, it's just . . . it's Jeremy Brewer!"

I almost tell her no, I will *not* scooch down a seat. This is *my* seat, and she's been dancing with Jeremy Brewer all night! Can't I have one bite of cake with my best friend at her bat mitzvah?

But Jeremy Brewer is here now, and she looks so excited to be near him. So happy and blushy, I could never say no to her.

"Sure," I say.

And even though the cake tastes like it was baked last week, I stuff my mouth as full of it as I can.

It's the only way to keep myself from crying.

Jew-ish

The party is almost over, and I couldn't be more ready to go home. Maybe, once we scrub the makeup off our faces and wash the party out of our hair, things will go back to normal.

I take my goody bag from the table and say goodbye to my friends. As we're walking away to find our parents, Lin stops me. "You're Jewish, too, right, Hannah? Are you also going to have a bat mitzvah?"

But before I get a chance to say, *No, my family isn't all that Jewish. Today was only my fifth time inside of a temple* ever! Shira interrupts.

"Of course Hannah isn't having a bat mitzvah!" She puts her arm around me and pulls me to her side. "Hannah's not *really* Jewish. Right, Hannah?"

And my face must

f

a

l

l

because Lin says, "It's okay, Hannah! It doesn't matter!"

And it's not that Shira is wrong, exactly, and it's not that she's saying anything I haven't said myself a million times, or anything different from what I was planning on saying to Lin right now. But there's something about the way she said it that just . . . bugs me.

I'm not *really* Jewish.

And maybe it's because Dad said I wasn't really Jewish this morning, and then he said it again at the temple.

Or maybe it's because Mom told me to "fix" my hair earlier today, or because it's frizzing up again now.

Or maybe it's because Shira brushed me off for her Hebrew school friend at the temple and for Jeremy Brewer during the slow dance.

And it's at least a little bit because she kissed him.

But these are pretty much the first words Shira has said to me all day, and they are about how I'm not *really* Jewish.

Well, I may not be really Jewish, but I felt something in that temple today. And who is Shira to say what I really am?

And so maybe that's why I say it.

Because I want it to be true.

Because it should be true.

Because I believe one day it *will* be true.

Or maybe I'm lying to myself, and I only say it because, when it comes down to it, I'm not happy for Shira at all.

I'm jealous.

"Actually," I say, "I *am* going to have a bat mitzvah. My parents said I could!"

It doesn't matter that now I have to find some way to convince my parents that I should have a bat mitzvah. It's worth it to see the shock on Shira's face.

Roots

My family is quiet on the way home. It's late, and everyone seems close to dozing off, but after the night I had, I don't think I could fall asleep even if I wanted to.

"Mom? Dad?"

Dad keeps his eyes on the road, and Mom picks her head up to look at me.

"Can I have a bat mitzvah?"

The car is suddenly so quiet, I wonder if I imagined asking the question.

"Why do you want a bat mitzvah all of a sudden?" Mom asks.

"You've never mentioned this before," says Dad.

"Seems like a ton of work for some elaborate social performance," Sam adds unnecessarily.

"Let her speak," says Grandma Mimi.

My head swirls with all the things I could say:

I want to have my first kiss in front of my whole class, and it was so cool when Shira spoke Hebrew, and I want to learn it too, and I want a big party with a fancy downtown cake, and also, I actually felt something kind of awesome when I sang along to the songs at the temple, and I'd like to feel that again.

Oh, and I kind of already said I was having one.

But something tells me none of those answers will get me to a yes. So instead I say, "Because I want to connect with my Jewish roots."

And there's a moment where everyone is thinking. Processing. Considering. And maybe

maybe

maybe

maybe

there's a chance they'll say yes . . .

. . . and they all burst out laughing.

Uprooted

"Never mind," I say. "I was just kidding."

Commitment

When I'm getting ready for bed, Grandma Mimi knocks on the door of my room. "I'm sorry, Hannah. I didn't mean to laugh at you. You caught me by surprise! If you want to have a bat mitzvah, if you want to make that commitment to God and your family and your community, well I think it's beautiful."

When she puts it that way, it does sound beautiful. Magical, even.

"When I was your age," Grandma Mimi continues, "girls didn't have bat mitzvahs. Only boys could read from the Torah. And oh! I wanted a bat mitzvah so much my teeth hurt! I wanted the party, sure, and the dancing and the cake, but that Torah . . . I've never seen anything so beautiful.

"Purple velvet, golden tassels, and parchment so fine I never once doubted that its words came straight from God. I wanted so much to read from the Torah, but that's not how things worked back then.

"And when my brother became a bar mitzvah, I was so jealous, I hid in a closet! That was the day I decided that if the rules didn't make sense, I'd rewrite them.

"Your mom's bat mitzvah was a beautiful day. I wish she loved being Jewish as much as I do, but it's complicated for her.

"She—

"Well—

"It's complicated."

"What happened between her and Aunt Yael?" I ask.

"I wish I could tell you, bubbelah," says Grandma Mimi. "But it's your mother's story, and when she's ready to talk about it, she will."

I don't know why I bother asking anymore. Mom gets all intense and sad whenever I bring it up, and when I ask anybody else, the answer I get is always some blend of "It's not my story to tell" and "It's none of your business."

"Just promise me one thing, Hannah." Grandma Mimi moves to leave my room, tugging at her Star of David necklace as she goes.

"Yeah?" I say, curling under the covers.

"If this is something you want," she says. "If you are committed to understanding your Jewish roots. To interrogating and questioning and wondering and wrestling with who you are and what it means to be Jewish, promise me that when it comes time for your big day"—she flicks off my lights—"don't waste your money on a cake that tastes like sand."

The Big Book of What's Cooking

The next day is Sunday, and even though it's one of those perfect fall days that actually feels like fall instead of too-late summer or too-early winter, I don't leave the house. I mean, I would have left the house if Shira wanted to go to the park with me, but when I messaged her, she saw it and didn't respond.

It's fine, though. She has family in town, so I'm sure she's spending her Sunday with them. And what better way to spend a fall day than with Sam and Grandma Mimi and the Big Book of What's Cooking?

The Big Book of What's Cooking is Grandma Mimi's binder of recipes. It's illegible, and not just because most of the recipes are written in pencil and faded with use. And not just because she wrote them as a little girl in her baby cursive chicken-scratch handwriting. And not just because there are seventy years of underlines and cross-outs, add-ons and insertions.

But because they're barely recipes at all.

They're notes.

Poems.

Scribbles.

Messages from young Miriam Rubenstein to old Grandma Mimi.

Secret codes passed from girl to grandma, child to adult, past to future.

Words only the author can read.

And her grandkids of course.

And today is the perfect day to crack open the book and whip out the recipe for Pretty Please Pie. It's my parents' favorite, so it's the perfect thing to make when trying to convince them of something. And after my failed attempt at getting bat mitzvah permission last night, Pretty Please Pie might be exactly what I need.

I'm rolling out piecrust on the counter while Grandma Mimi dices apples and Sam wrestles with our famously stubborn food processor. "When I start my own bakery," Sam says, "we're going to have all new appliances."

"Hey." Grandma Mimi waves her peeler at Sam. "Be grateful you have appliances at all, eh?"

Sam flicks our food processor on and off and on again, groaning when it doesn't start. "I hear National Hobart has state-of-the-art kitchens at their culinary school." He shrugs, all casual, as if this is a random, inconsequential fact he happened to remember at the moment.

"Oh they do, do they?" Mom says.

"Yep. Their applications are open for next year. I think I may apply."

"Yeah, right." Dad laughs from the kitchen table. "We didn't spend a small fortune sending you to a math and science school so you could make pies for a living."

The mood in the kitchen, so bright and cheerful a moment ago, suddenly turns sour. Ever since Sam was little, he's said he wants to start his own bakery one day. But now that he's a senior and college applications are right around the corner, owning a bakery has gone from being a cute thing he used to dream about to an actual possibility. And Dad, our resident financial . . .

. . . something-or-other . . .

. . . isn't too happy about it.

"Opening a bakery is a massive waste of your potential," Dad says, as if this were the most obvious fact in the world.

I let out an exaggerated sigh. "Do we have to do this now? We were having such a nice day."

But no one seems to hear me.

"Luckily," says Sam, "it's not your call what I do with my future."

"I think it *is* my call, actually, since you're my kid and I'm the one paying for it—"

"Richard," Mom cuts in. "There's no harm in him applying."

"Of course there is," Dad says. "If he gets in, he's going to want to go. And I'm *not* paying for my kid to learn how to bake cakes."

"And what is so wrong with baking cakes?" Sam says. "Not corporate enough for you?"

Dad's about to bite back. I can already see his shoulders tensing with a reply, but before he can get a word out, Grandma Mimi snaps her fingers. "Oy," she says. "Quit your kvetching, eh?" Then she looks at Sam, and it's only because I'm standing near him that I see it. She winks at him and mouths the words, "I got you."

And Sam seems skeptical, but he shrugs the fight off anyway. "Whatever," he says, turning our food processor on and off one more time before it whirs to life. "Finally!" he says, heading over to the pantry to grab the sugar, where he adds a handful to the bowl, saving a pinch to sprinkle in my back-to-bushy hair.

"Hey!" I shout. I grab Sam's hand and try to redirect it to his own hair, but I can barely reach his chin, much less his scalp, and suddenly Grandma Mimi's laughing, and Sam is laughing, which means I laugh too, and it's not long before even Mom and Dad are laughing, and just like that, any worries I had—of Shira and bat mitzvahs and whether Sam should go to culinary school—melt away like butter in a piecrust.

Piecrust

<u>By weight:</u>

　　3 parts flour (all purpose)

　　2 parts fat (butter, vegetable oil, shortening)

　　1 part liquid (~~cold~~ water)
　　　　　　　　^ICED

　　pinch of salt

For tender crust, soft and chewy —

　　liquid fat, ~~incoprate~~ incorporate fully.

For flaky crust, crisp and warm —

　　~~freeze~~ freeze fat first

leave chunks in dough

Press into pie-tin and freeze before filling.

<u>Remember:</u>

　　Melts in the oven, melts in your mouth.

Pretty Please Pie

The pie turns out perfectly, and even though Mom is a scientist and is always saying there's no such thing as luck, sometimes I feel like a successful pie is a sign of other good things to come.

"Pretty please can I have a bat mitzvah?"

"Hannah," Mom says, exasperated. "We already told you no."

"Dad?"

"I'm not debating this with you anymore."

"Ugh!" I groan. "Give me one good reason why not!"

"Because we don't even go to temple!" And before I can jump in to say I *want* to go to temple, Mom puts her hand up. "Bat mitzvahs are also expensive, and they take years to prepare, for the parents as well as the kids. Besides, bat mitzvahs are supposed to mean something. They're not just big parties, even though, after last night, it feels like that."

"I know," I say. "But it's not fair that you can say no to something like this just because you're my parents. This is what Jewish kids do. And I'm Jewish. Aren't I?"

Mom looks at Dad, and Dad looks at Mom. Grandma Mimi and Sam, who have been noisily cleaning up the kitchen while I argue with my parents, stop banging pots and pans together. And all at once I know I'm about to get the answer.

The *real* answer.

The answer that's so bitter, no amount of Pretty Please Pie could ever sweeten it.

Mom is the one who says it, with a sigh like an apology, but from the way Dad is poking holes in the crust of his pie, I know she speaks for both of them when she says, "Well, no, Hannah. Honestly, you're not. You're not Jewish."

And I want to fight back, to say I am Jewish, because Grandma Mimi is Jewish, which means Mom is Jewish even if she doesn't believe she is anymore. And Grandma Mimi has told me that Judaism passes through the mom, not the dad, so it doesn't matter that Dad was raised Catholic. That's not what it means to be Jewish. Being Jewish means—

"That's not true," Sam says, butting in. "It's not true that Hannah isn't Jewish. That any of us aren't."

"Thank you!" I say. "Someone is on my side!"

Sam puts down the pot he's scrubbing. "We can joke about being fake Jews all we want, but we can't claim we aren't Jewish without also acknowledging that any one of us, including Dad, if we're being honest, would have been Jewish enough for Hitler."

And just like that, I wish he had never said anything.

"Sam!" says Grandma Mimi.

Mom curses under her breath, and without so much as a snarky comment, Dad lets his head fall into his open palm.

"No one is saying it, but it's true," Sam continues. "Do we think Nazis give a crap how we feel about our Judaism? People ask me if I'm Jewish before they hear my last name, so it's not like I have the luxury of hiding it. And especially now, with what we see on the news every day and what's going on in our own backyard. Nathan Fulweiler goes to temple in Lincoln Park, and he said their synagogue got tagged last month. And—"

"Tagged?" I interrupt.

"Sam, maybe we shouldn't—" Mom starts.

"No. This is important!" Sam says. "It concerns her. It concerns all of us."

I'm not sure how exactly this concerns us, since, as everyone has been reminding me all day, we don't belong to a temple. But hey, I'm not complaining, as long as someone explains it to me.

"It means vandalized," Sam says. "Hit with graffiti. Apparently it happens all the time, but it gets brushed under the rug because it's too ugly to deal with—and it's not like there's any way to figure out who did it. And—"

"Sam." Grandma Mimi says his name almost at a whisper, but it's enough to get him to step off his soapbox. Because Grandma Mimi doesn't look happy. "There are many horrible things in the world," she says. "But we don't define ourselves by who hates us."

Sam nods and puts away the dish he's drying. "That's fair. But it's something to acknowledge, anyway. We don't always get a choice in who we are."

And with that, the room grows quiet and we all shift back to what we were doing before Sam butted into my conversation, except now everyone is tense and quiet. Mom and Dad aren't even touching their pie.

So thanks a lot, Sam, because it's your fault the bat mitzvah conversation is officially over.

Eavesdropping

That night, I'm in my room, on my laptop, researching ways of giving myself a bat mitzvah. But the more I learn, the more I realize I'm going to need *someone's* help. I need someone to teach me the prayers, someone to tell me which songs to sing in which order, and the only way I'll ever have access to a temple to perform it all in is if I have a rabbi on my side.

But where am I going to find one of those?

That's when I hear Mom's voice from downstairs, floating through the vent in my bedroom floor.

"What is she asking for?" Mom says. "If all she wants is a thirteenth birthday party, we can throw her a thirteenth birthday party."

"Why don't you ask Hannah," Grandma Mimi says. "What does a bat mitzvah mean to her?"

"But it's not her decision," Mom says. "No matter how you look at it, a bat mitzvah is a religious act, and I get to determine the religion of my own child."

"Maybe Judaism isn't about religion to her."

"Oh, come on!" Uh-oh. Dad's weighing in. "Are you trying to tell me Judaism isn't a religion?"

"It is," Grandma Mimi says. "And it isn't. But isn't the point of being a bat mitzvah that Hannah is old enough to come up with her own definition of what it means to be Jewish?"

"My daughter is *not* a bat mitzvah, because my daughter is *not* Jewish!"

"But she is," says Grandma Mimi.

"She isn't if I say she isn't!"

"That's not how it works, Liat."

"How does it work then, Mom? Please enlighten me on who gets to determine whether my own daughter is Jewish or not. You said we don't let people who hate us decide who we are, but does it work differently with our families—with the people who love us? Do *they* get to decide who we are? Well, I have news for you, Mom. The only one who gets to decide who I am is me."

"Shouldn't your daughter get to decide for herself, too?"

Mom doesn't have a response to that, and if I were keeping score, I would add one point for team bat mitzvah. But when Mom speaks again, her voice is soft and wobbly, and there's no arguing with a crying Mom. "I just don't want Judaism in the house," she says, and I wonder again, for the millionth time, why she feels so strongly.

"I know after what happened with Yael, Judaism left a bad taste in your mouth," Grandma Mimi says.

Dad snorts. "That's the understatement of the century."

"Be that as it may, Hannah's growing up. Maybe if you explained to her why this is so hard on you, she might understand better. And maybe it would help you to move on! I've always thought—"

"I know what you've thought, Mom. Please spare me the lecture on forgiveness."

"Even so. Talk to your daughter, Liat. She may surprise you."

It's quiet for a moment, but then I hear footsteps, and I have just enough time to minimize the DIY bat mitzvah windows on my laptop screen before Mom knocks on my door. "Can I come in?" she asks.

"Sure, Mom," I say. "What's up?"

"I wanted to talk to you," she says. "I know you think it's unfair that we said you couldn't have a bat mitzvah, but I wanted to explain a little bit about why."

I nod and try to make my voice sound casual. "Okay." But it's hard to be casual because this is finally it! I've been waiting seven years to learn why Mom doesn't talk to Aunt Yael anymore, and I finally will!

"You see, Judaism—religion—it's not just about saying some fancy words and baking rugelach. Religion is a way of thinking about the world. I know you've only ever seen the good parts of being Jewish, and I know you won't believe me when I say this, but religion isn't always a good thing. It can be bad as easily as good. Evil, even, and—"

"Evil?" I raise my eyebrows at her. Is this still about her and Aunt Yael? "You can't be serious."

"I am serious. Religion can be cruel. Religion can be spiteful, and it can be divisive and it can brainwash people into believing those who are different from them are less worthy of love. It breaks families apart. And countries, too! Do you know how many countries right now are in the throes of a religion-based civil war?"

"Mom?" I try to keep my voice calm. "I think you're being a little dramatic. I'm not trying to start a war or join a cult. I just want to have a party."

"That's exactly it," Mom says. "You want a party. You haven't given any thought to what it actually means to be Jewish, and I think if you did, you might discover being Jewish isn't all that great."

I know she's dancing around it. I know she's inches away from telling me what happened between her and Aunt Yael, but before she can say the words, she stops herself. "I'm going to go to bed. And when I wake up, I don't want to hear anything more about bat mitzvahs. Okay?"

I nod, and Mom kisses me good night and turns off my light.

But as soon as my room is dark, all I can see is the memory of being in that temple.

I remember looking around the room and seeing Shira so proud and confident, Grandma Mimi lost in song, and Aunt Yael full of something

so

    so

       so

I dunno.

Something.

There's no way something that powerful could be evil, any more than someone like my Aunt Yael could be evil.

And so with that, I've decided.

My mom is wrong, and I'm going to prove it to her.

Operation bat mitzvah is a go.

And I think I know who my rabbi should be.

Icing

Every morning, while Grandma Mimi drives me to Shira's, I watch the houses we pass, looking for anything that's changed since I last saw them. We live in one of those neighborhoods that's been basically the same as long as I can remember, so when I do see something different, it sticks out. One house started a garden, and now every week they have some new flash of pink and green. One big house seems like it's always under construction, and now they're adding a new bedroom. And last month this other house painted its front door a bright sunshine yellow.

And sometimes, if I'm not paying attention, the people inside the houses change too.

We're in front of Shira's house now, and she's coming out of her front door, but for a second I wonder if maybe we're at the wrong address, because the person I'm seeing now can't possibly be Shira.

She's wearing a dress, which she's *never* worn to school before, since she says dresses make her legs cold. And instead of carrying her normal purple JanSport backpack, she's carrying this purse that's so small, there's no way it can carry all her books.

Plus, Shira's face doesn't look like it normally does. Instead, it's frosted. Red, blue, brown, blush, eye shadow, mascara, and all of it thicker than royal icing.

But when she comes into the car, I pretend I don't see any difference. Why should it matter what Shira's wearing to school? But she makes it hard, because when I offer her a slice of Pretty Please Pie, she says, "Oh, I can't. It would smear my lip-gloss."

No Thank You Pie

Breakfast doesn't taste half as good when I eat it by myself.

Point of No Return

Something about Shira today is off, and I don't just mean the way she's dressed. All through the car ride I feel like I'm talking to a brick wall. She keeps typing on her new iPhone, fixing her hair in the camera, and talking to me as little as possible.

"Are you okay?" I ask once we get to school. "What's wrong?"

But Shira shrugs and says, "It's nothing."

I don't believe it's nothing, so all day I try to make her feel better. I tell her how great her new earrings look, and I tell her I love her dress. I make a big deal about the A she gets on her math test, because I remember she was nervous about it, and at lunch, when she pulls out her leftover Her Cake, I ask if I can have a bite.

Shira must know that it's not really about the cake, because she calls me out. "Why do you need to taste mine, Hannah? You'll have your own in six months anyway when you have *your* bat mitzvah!"

That's when I realize why she's acting so weird.

She's *mad* at me!

Because I said I was going to have a bat mitzvah!

But that doesn't seem fair, since there's no reason I shouldn't be allowed to have one. I mean, except that my parents won't let me, but Shira doesn't know that. Why would she care if I have a bat mitzvah?

Is that why she ignored my messages yesterday? She was mad at me? Why didn't she just *tell* me that? We could have talked it out!

But in the time it takes me to figure out what to say, everyone around us has already started talking.

"I didn't know Hannah was having a bat mitzvah!"

"Me neither! Since when?"

"I didn't know you were even, like, eligible."

"Oh my god, Chris, that is *so* rude."

"Yeah, you can't just say that!"

"Jeez, sorry, okay?"

And throughout it all, Shira keeps giving me this intense look, like she's trying to read my mind. And I guess she is, in a way, because she says, "You're not really having a bat mitzvah, are you? You've never talked about it before. I didn't know you even cared about that sort of thing."

And from the way everyone is looking at me right now, I know this is my last chance.

To back out.

To put things back to normal.

To add a little sugar and a little butter and turn this mistake into a cupcake.

Now is my chance to make up an excuse about how my parents took it back this morning. How they thought I meant a thirteenth birthday party bat mitzvah, not a *bat mitzvah* bat mitzvah.

Why would I want a bat mitzvah?

I'm not *really* Jewish!

Who cares about that tingly feeling I got at the temple?

Or that bits of Hebrew have soaked into my brain like sugared syrup into a pound cake.

It's not worth making my best friend angry, and my parents already said no anyway.

I should back out.

I should definitely back out.

I might have backed out, if not for what Shira says next.

"I mean, Hannah, you're not even *really* Jewish."

And that's when I decide.

If this is my last chance to back out,

I'm not taking it.

I won't back out.

I can't back out.

I'm having a bat mitzvah, no matter what.

Sour

"Yes, Shira, I am having a bat mitzvah. And you're right. I don't need to taste your leftover cake because I brought enough pie for everybody to share."

I think this might be the first time Pretty Please Pie has ever made someone mad.

Proceeding as Unusual

Shira is late to social studies, which means the seat next to me is empty when the new kid, I think her name is Victoria, comes in and asks to sit there.

"Sorry," I say. "This is where Shira usually sits."

But without Shira physically sitting in the chair beside me, I must be about as assertive as lime Jell-O. The new kid doesn't seem to hear me. She's too busy laughing at something on her phone, and then I hear her mumble "Just two hundred and fourteen more days" before putting the phone in her backpack. I resist the urge to ask her what's going to happen in two hundred and fourteen days. I don't want her to think I'm spying on her.

Just then, Shira comes in. I mouth the words "I'm sorry" at her and make a sour face in the direction of the new kid sitting in her usual seat. I expect Shira to make the same face back to me, but she doesn't. She doesn't even seem to care that someone else is sitting next to me. She just shrugs and mouths "It's fine" before walking straight toward Jeremy Brewer.

As if that's where she'd rather be anyway.

Victoria

When Ms. Shapiro, our social studies teacher, comes into class, she takes a dry erase marker out of the tray and writes our daily partner discussion topic on the board: "What is the most valuable object in your possession?" All I can think about is how I should be having this conversation with Shira.

See, Shira and I play a game where we each answer the daily question as if we were the other person. Like, for this one, I would talk about the baby blankets Shira's grandparents gave her on the day she was born. I'd talk about how they've been through the washing machine so many times they no longer look much like two blankets but more like one clump of rags, and I'd remind her that she sleeps with them every night anyway.

I'm not sure what she'd say for me, but that's the fun of our game. Sometimes your best friend knows you better than you know yourself.

Shira's already talking to Jeremy Brewer, but I doubt she's talking about her baby blankets. That's the sort of thing she can only talk about with me.

"Hello?" says Victoria, snapping her fingers to get my attention. "You there?"

"Sorry," I say, rolling my eyes at Shira and Jeremy Brewer.

But Victoria must think I'm rolling my eyes at her. She says, "You know, I'm not exactly thrilled to be doing this either. At my old school, we didn't have to do stupid partner discussion topics like we do at your school."

It takes everything in me not to make a lemon face. Isn't this her school too? And it's not like I'm the one who came up with the idea of partner discussion topics, so why is she making me feel like this is my fault somehow?

"These discussion topics *are* stupid," I say.

Victoria blows her bangs out of her face and says, "At least we agree on that."

Recipe for Victoria

Mix together
one (1) black hoodie
    with some logo on it
    that looks like a band I've never heard of
one (1) black pair of jeans
    with rips on the knees
two (2) black boots
    with laces reaching practically to her knee rips
one (1) purple streak in her hair
    breaking up the otherwise head-to-toe
    blackness.

Valuable

"I guess I'll go first," says Victoria, looking at her watch. "The most valuable object in my possession is my flute."

She closes her mouth and gives me a look like now it's my turn to talk, but we have five minutes to fill up with this stupid question, so no way is she going to make *me* talk for that whole time.

"Why is your flute so valuable to you?" I ask.

Victoria shrugs. "I guess because my mom got it as a wedding present from her family back in Guatemala, and she used to play for my dad, back when she—" She clears her throat. "A long time ago." She stops talking again and looks at me once more, like she's finished with her turn.

But only one minute has passed, so I ask her a follow-up question. "Do you play at all?"

"A little," she says. "I used to take lessons back when we lived in Miami, but it seems like a waste of time to try to find a teacher here, since we're going to be moving back there at the end of the year."

"Moving back?"

"Yep. In two hundred and fourteen days." Victoria rolls her eyes. "I mean, *technically* we might end up staying, but my dad promised me that if I still hate it here at the end of the year, he won't make me stay. And I don't see how I could ever *not* hate it, because pretty much my whole life is back there. Plus, it's freezing here all the time."

"Hey!" I say. "It's not that cold. I didn't even wear a coat to school today!"

She raises an eyebrow at the jacket I have draped around my chair.

"That's not a coat, that's a jacket," I say, and Victoria smirks at me. "Wait until the summer," I continue. "Then you'll be too hot."

"Doubt it," Victoria says, suppressing a laugh. "What about you? What's your"—she makes air quotes with her fingers—" 'most valuable possession'?"

"Hmm . . ." I say, stalling for time. I don't have a great answer for this one. I mean, I have a stuffed koala I got when I was four that I'd be sad if I lost, but it's not like Shira's baby blankets that she sleeps with every night.

Mom got me a bracelet for my tenth birthday that I wear when I'm supposed to dress up. It's probably the most expensive gift I've ever gotten, but if it got lost, I don't think I'd notice.

What would Shira say if she were answering for me? She'd probably try to think of what I would be the saddest to lose.

What would be the hardest to replace if it ever got lost? What couldn't I live without?

"The Big Book of What's Cooking," I say. "It's this book of recipes my grandmother's been collecting since she was little. We cook something from there practically every day. Lots of cakes, cookies, pies. A lot of Jewish recipes from when she was little."

"Oh!" says Victoria, her voice perking up. "I didn't know you were Jewish."

"Well . . . I'm not. Not really."

"What makes you say that?" She clutches at something at the nape of her neck.

"I mean, I am," I say. "Sort of. My mom's mom is Jewish anyway, and I know if your mom is Jewish, you're Jewish."

Victoria blows air out of her nose. "You know the whole Jewish-blood-comes-from-the-mom thing is misogynist garbage, right? It's only the mom because you couldn't 'prove' who a baby's father was. As if being Jewish is all about genetics anyway."

Victoria sounds like Sam when she says this, but even though I have no idea what she's referring to, I nod. "Yeah, of course I knew all that. Obviously."

She smiles a little bit, as if she knows I'm lying, but before she has a chance to say anything else, Ms. Shapiro flickers the lights. Discussions are over, but as I'm turning back to the front of the room, I see Victoria tuck whatever she was clutching back into her sweatshirt.

Friendless

That afternoon when Grandma Mimi picks us up, we are in the car for approximately ten seconds before Shira opens her big mouth.

"Hannah, I'm *so* excited for your bat mitzvah!"

Suddenly my heart

f

a

l

l

s

and I can practically picture my future stretching out before me. A future where Grandma Mimi says *What bat mitzvah?* and Shira says *Hah! I knew you weren't having one! You lied to me! Best friendship* over!

But Grandma Mimi surprises me. "I'm also excited!" she says. "In fact, I'm more excited for Hannah to become a bat mitzvah than I am for anything else in the world."

The rest of the ride is quiet, almost eerily so, but no amount of awkward silence can deflate the bubble of joy that grew in my stomach with Grandma Mimi's words. And Shira is barely out of the car before I ask, "Did you mean that? You're excited for my bat mitzvah?"

With one hand Grandma Mimi pinches her Star of David necklace, and with the other she takes my hand in hers.

"Of course I meant it! Why would you ask that?"

"For starters," I say, "I'm not allowed to have a bat mitzvah."

"Feh!" She waves her hand in the air. "What is this *allowed*?"

"Mom and Dad said—"

"Hannah, a Jewish girl becomes a bat mitzvah when she turns thirteen, no matter what her parents *allow*. Can you forbid someone from growing up?"

The bubble of joy bursts.

Grandma Mimi isn't talking about having a bat mitzvah.

She's talking about becoming one.

What good is that?

"Besides," Grandma Mimi adds, "if my Hannah wants a ceremony, something to commemorate her becoming a Jewish adult, she knows where to find me."

All of a sudden the bubble is back, and I know now is my chance to ask Grandma Mimi for her help. "What if I told you I had an idea?"

I tell her what it is, and she smiles. "I was hoping you'd ask me that."

"So you're in?"

"Not only am I in," she says, "but I called her on Sunday. She says you can start Thursday after school. But promise me one thing." She lifts a finger into the air. "Let me be the one to tell your mother."

I nod, surprised that Grandma Mimi is encouraging me to keep something from my parents. "That's fine, but . . . why?"

She kisses the tops of my fingers and says, "If we handle this delicately, it could be the way your mother learns to forgive."

Frying

The next morning, I wake up early.

One hour early, in order to de-

f r i z z

my

lint ball

dust bunny

cotton candy

hair.

So I set my alarm for before sunrise, and I borrow Mom's
hair straightener.

And before I know it, it's working.

My hair is

sleek

elegant

glamorous.

And the rotten egg smell of frying hair is totally worth it.

Because I look awesome.

Delicate

Anybody who ever said
French macarons are the most delicate thing
you'll ever create
has never created
a lie.

Mine is half-baked
full of holes
and hot air
and if I'm not careful
it's all going to fall

flat.

Recipe for the Bat Mitzvah That I Tell Everyone About

Mix Together:

"Of course everyone's invited!"

"Theme? Candy Castle."

"No! Alice in Wonderland."

"Um . . . April sixteenth."

"Four-layer cake!"

"No! Five-layer cake!"

"Make-your-own-sundae bar!"

"Of course there will be dancing!"

"Oh, my parents? Yeah, my parents are *definitely* excited."

Aunt Yael

I'm not lying to my friends. At least, not exactly. I'm telling a pre-truth.

Because I will be having a bat mitzvah, and why shouldn't my cake be five layers! And sure, my parents aren't onboard *right now,* but they will be once Grandma Mimi talks to Mom like she promised she would.

Every day this week I ask Grandma Mimi if she's talked to Mom yet, and every day she says, "This subject is delicate, and it's going to take patience. I'll talk to her when the time is right, and until then, you focus on your part in all of this — studying."

But it's hard to focus on studying when I don't have anything yet to study. I have to wait until Thursday for my first lesson, but that's fine because Shira and I seem back to normal. Or at least back to some sort of new normal. She's still frosting her face and sitting next to Jeremy Brewer in social studies, and he's become a permanent fixture at our lunch table. But at least on the trips to and from school, when it's just me and Shira, we're the same as always. I even went over to her house after school on Tuesday to do some homework and ended up staying so late playing Boggle that Mom and Dad let me sleep over.

By the time Thursday afternoon rolls around, I'm starting to think this bat mitzvah thing might work out. My parents think I'm staying late at school tonight to work on a long-term group project, but I'll actually be in Bronzeville for my first night of Hebrew school.

After Grandma Mimi drops Shira off, we leave our neighborhood, and before I know it, we arrive at Aunt Yael's house.

"Go on," says Grandma Mimi. "I'll wait here until you're done."

"You're not coming in?" I ask.

Grandma Mimi shakes her head. "This is all you, bubbeleh."

I open the car door and walk to the building. I know I've been here before, when I was little, but I don't remember it. I find the doorbell, ring it, and after a few seconds I hear my aunt's voice.

"Hannah?"

I take a deep breath. "It's me," I say. And then?

Buzzzzzzzzzzzz.

I walk up the stairs and don't even have a chance to knock on her apartment door before it's swinging open and I'm wrapped in a hug from a woman I haven't talked to since I was five years old.

I'm in my Aunt Yael's kitchen.

Recipe for Aunt Yael

Mix together
High-heeled shoes
and long, frizzy hair
    worn wrapped up in a cinnamon bun
    on top of her head.
one (1) Star of David necklace
    matching her mom's
one (1) wall full of books with titles like
    Souls on Fire
    and *A Child of Faith*
    and *God Is a Woman.*
Bake for forty-something years
and when you're done
mix with one (1) recipe for
    Hannah Malfa-Adler.
Then decorate with
one (1) facial expression shared among
two (2) people, made of
    one (1) part nerves
    two (2) parts joy.

Ingredients in a Bat Mitzvah

Her kitchen is cozy, like the inside of a kitchen should be.

"Uh . . . hi," I say. I feel awkward, I guess. What do you say to someone you haven't spoken to in seven years?

But Aunt Yael is talking a million miles a minute while hunting for something in the kitchen. "My mom—your Grandma Mimi—she tells me you want my help to prepare for your bat mitzvah. Well, I think that's a great idea, and I'm happy to help. In fact, I've always wondered if you kids would want to pursue Judaism, and I'm thrilled to be part of it. Aha!" She holds up a Tupperware bowl, which must have been what she was hunting for. She takes off the lid, and the entire room fills with the smell of fall.

Butter

and chocolate,

with a hint of cinnamon.

And just like that, I know I'm exactly where I belong.

I tell her everything.

About Shira and Mom and Dad and how they all said I'm not really Jewish.

About how Sam said I was Jewish, but only because Hitler would have thought so.

About how that made Grandma Mimi upset, and she thinks I'm Jewish because she's Jewish. But Victoria didn't seem to think genetics mattered.

About how I want a bat mitzvah, and how I told my friends I was definitely going to have one, even though my parents said I couldn't.

About how it's not really a lie, right? Because I *am* going to have a bat mitzvah. And my parents *will* be okay with it once Grandma Mimi talks to them.

And finally, I tell her all I need is a little bit of help to make it possible.

"It can't be that hard," I say. "I learn some prayers, read some Hebrew, write an essay about what it means to be Jewish, sing some songs—or are those prayers too?

"And that's it, right?

"That's all I need to do?"

Aunt Yael looks at me with an expression I swear she stole from Mom's face. "Is that all you want to do?"

I nod.

"You want to learn your Torah portion, say some prayers, give a speech, and you're done?"

I nod again.

"You know a bat mitzvah can be anything you want, right? It can be meaningful. It can be about you."

I nod a third time.

"But you want to memorize some prayers and have a party like what you saw Shira do."

I nod.

"Well, I want this bat mitzvah to be about what you want. So if that's what you want"—she claps her hands—"I guess that's what we're going to do!"

Aunt Yael stands up and rummages through her bookshelf. "I know I put it . . . somewhere . . . ah! Here we go!" She takes a heavy-looking folder off the top shelf and flips through it, plunking it on the table when she finds the right page.

ט	ח	ז	ו	ה	ד	ג	ב	א
Teit	Cheit	Zayin	Vav	Hei	Dalet	Gimel	Bet	Alef
(T)	(Ch)	(Z)	(V,O,U)	(H)	(D)	(G)	(B/V)	(Silent)
ס	נ	ן	מ	ם	ל	כ	כ	י
Samekh	Nun	Nun	Mem	Mem	Lamed	Khaf	Kaf	Yod
(S)	(N)	(N)	(M)	(M)	(L)	(Kh)	(K/Kh)	(Y)
ת	ש	ר	ק	ץ	צ	ף	פ	ע
Tav	Shin	Reish	Qof	Tzadei	Tzadei	Fe	Pei	Ayin
(T/S)	(Sh/S)	(R)	(Q)	(Tz)	(Tz)	(F)	(P/F)	(Silent)

"It's the alphabet!" Aunt Yael says. "Or . . . the alef-bet, more technically."

I study the page in front of me. I've seen the letters before, of course, but this is the first time I'm actually *seeing* them. And now that I'm paying attention, I'm not sure how Shira was able to read this stuff.

First of all, about half the letters look like backwards *r*'s, and the other half look like backwards *c*'s, and a whole lot of them look like boxes, and I can't tell most of them apart from one another—and somehow I'm supposed to read this?

"Umm . . ." I say. "Thank you?"

Aunt Yael laughs. "Don't worry too much. You have plenty of time to study at home before your next lesson."

Studying?

At home?

I kind of thought this would be . . .

. . . like . . .

. . . it.

I'd come in once a week, learn my Hebrew, bake for six months, and out would pop a bat mitzvah.

Of course I don't say that. The last thing I want is for Aunt Yael to think I'm not up for this. But the longer I stay in her kitchen, the more I feel like maybe I'm *not* up for this. On top of the already-confusing chart of Hebrew letters she's given me to take home, she hands me six books, two packets, seven loose-leaf pages, and four three-ring binders, each heavier than the last.

"We'll start by learning your Torah portion," Aunt Yael says, leafing through one of the binders, "since that will take the most time. You have an April birthday, so you'll be reading from Leviticus. Now, technically, your Torah portion should combine *Behar* and *Bechukotai,* but I don't see any reason to double your workload, so we'll just be learning *Behar,* and you're in luck again, because Rosh Hashanah just happened, and now it's the year 5782, which is a *Shmita,* so *Behar* is highly relevant."

I nod along, like I understood any of what she said, and Aunt Yael hands me a packet that has Hebrew written on the right-hand side and English written on the left. She says it's my Torah portion, so I guess that means it's *Behar.* I add it to my already full backpack.

"Okay," she says at the end of our lesson. "Before you go, I want you to listen to something." She motions me over to her laptop, and I follow. Aunt Yael pulls up an audio clip labeled with some backwards *r*'s and backwards *c*'s like the ones on the chart she showed me. "I'm going to send you some audio clips for you to study on your own, but this one in particular I want you to hear now. You're going to love it."

"Can't wait," I say.

I know I swore I was up for all this, that I *wanted* to do the work everyone's been warning me about, but now that I'm here, my back aching under the weight of all the books I'm supposed to read, I'm not sure if I'd be able to learn all this even if I had the rest of my life to study, much less six months.

So why am I doing this?

But all of a sudden Aunt Yael's kitchen fills with the most beautiful sound I've ever heard.

It's a woman, singing something brand-new in a language I don't understand but somehow sounds familiar. The melody jumps and leaps, swoops and soars, resonating like some long-forgotten recipe.

And it's gorgeous.

"What is this?" I ask.

Aunt Yael smiles. "It's your Torah portion," she says. "*Behar.* Six months from now, this will be you."

Keeping My Cool

"How was it?" Grandma Mimi asks when I get into the car.

I try to keep calm, but I can't help but throw my arms in the air and shout, "I'm going to have a real bat mitzvah!"

The Letter

Nothing can get me down the whole ride home.

I'm going to have a real bat mitzvah!

Not the traffic.

I'm going to have a real bat mitzvah!

Not Grandma Mimi turning on the classical station when I would rather listen to literally anything else.

I'm going to have a real bat mitzvah!

Not the fact that it's almost six o'clock and I haven't started my homework.

I'm going to have a real bat mitzvah!

And when we get home, it gets even better. I'm greeted by the smell of some fruity, chocolatey concoction. Definitely a Sam experiment.

I'm going to have a real—

Then I hear shouts coming from the living room.

"I can't believe you went behind my back!"

"It's not like I needed a permission slip to apply!"

I look at Grandma Mimi, and her expression matches my own. "What's going on?" I ask. "What happened?"

But Grandma Mimi doesn't need to say anything. As soon as I see the letter on the kitchen table, I know what happened.

Dear Samuel,

Thank you for your interest in The Pastry Program at the National Hobart School of Culinary Arts, and congratulations on taking this important step toward advancing your education!
In order to prepare the rest of your application, we need the following information . . .

Every good baker knows there are some flavors that just don't mix. And for our family, those flavors have always been Dad and Sam. They're opposites, peanut butter and caviar, but this?

This is a whole new level for them.

"It's *my* life," Sam shouts from the living room.

"And you're *my* son," Dad responds.

"I don't like this," I whisper to Grandma Mimi. "Isn't there something we can do?"

She puts her arm around me. "Don't you think I saved some rugelach for this exact situation?"

She unearths some leftover cookies from last weekend and throws them on a plate. She stands in the doorway that sits between the kitchen and the living room and calls, "Richard!

Sam!" She plunks the cookies on the coffee table between them, right in front of their faces. "Eat up! You're only angry because you're hungry. This will tide you over until I make dinner." And just like that, their faces soften, calmed by the cookies.

I can't help but think how thankful I am for Grandma Mimi. I wonder if she winked at Sam again, told him she'd handle Dad, like she told me she would be the one to tell Mom about Aunt Yael. I don't know how she'll convince Dad that Sam should go to culinary school any more than I know how she'll convince Mom that I should study for my bat mitzvah with Aunt Yael. But I trust her. She'll figure it out.

Because if Dad is peanut butter and Sam is caviar, then Grandma Mimi is a saltine cracker.

The only thing that goes well with both.

Studying

That night, I study.

Or, at least, I try.

I can barely tell these letters apart when I've got two of them right next to each other, much less when I draw them out onto flash cards.

And it doesn't help that some letters are drawn in two different ways, so they look different but are really the same, and other letters have two different sounds combined into one letter, so they look the same but are really different.

Even when I switch to reading the English translation, my brain fuzzes. I know *Behar* has something to do with farming laws, and the numbers six and seven appear over and over again. But no matter how many times I read it, the words don't stick in my head.

I try to study, but my brain keeps picturing Shira sitting with Jeremy Brewer in social studies, and remembering Sam and Dad's fight rattling our walls. The English letters blur, the Hebrew letters blur, and eventually I give up for the night. I crawl into bed and close my eyes, picturing myself six months from now, in front of my friends and family, somehow deciphering these Hebrew letters and having a perfect bat mitzvah.

I fall asleep to the sound of *Behar* in my ears.

The next morning, I follow the houses that line the road on the way to Shira's, watching for anything that's changed in the last twenty-four hours. The house with the big gardens in the front yard planted something green last night. The house with all the construction is putting up a new fence in their front yard. And the house with the yellow door has one of those fall wreaths hanging around its peephole. But even with all these changes to keep my brain busy, I find myself thinking about last night at Aunt Yael's, and all I want is to talk to Shira about it. I want to tell her about speaking with my aunt for the first time in seven years, and how I'm going behind my parents' backs to do this bat mitzvah thing. And I want to tell her Aunt Yael made rugelach that tasted like *our* rugelach, and it made me feel like I was exactly where I needed to be.

But if I told Shira I was lying to my parents, I know what she'd say. *You wouldn't have to lie about having a bat mitzvah if you were really Jewish. Your parents should be going with you to Hebrew school and helping you practice your Torah portion. Just like my parents did for me.*

No. I have to hide this from Shira. She wouldn't understand.

But even though I'm keeping a secret, I'm in a good mood. So when Shira finally gets settled in the car, I say, "Shira! Wanna do something tonight?"

And maybe things are going to be okay between us, because her eyes light up. "Sure!" she says. "Shabbat dinner?"

And I smile.

"Shabbat dinner!"

Getting Along

I can't wait for Shabbat dinner that night, because Shabbat dinners with me and Shira are special. They're a just-for-us kind of thing. Shira's parents always say they're supposed to be for family only, but I'm always welcome because I *am* family.

Shira's still sitting with Jeremy Brewer in social studies today, but I can get through that. Tonight it's just going to be me and her.

Today's social studies discussion question is "What is your biggest fear?" and I'm once again partnered with Victoria — or Vee, as she asked me to call her.

I wonder what Shira will answer for this one. If I were answering for her, I'd probably say clowns, since we watched *It* this past Halloween, even though our parents said it was a bad idea. I thought the whole movie was silly, but the next morning Shira told me that she had nightmares so bad she didn't think she'd ever be able to go to the circus again.

Maybe after Shabbat dinner tonight, we'll go back to being discussion partners.

"You first," Vee says to me.

"All right." This is an easy one. "Spiders."

Vee snorts.

"What? Why is that funny?"

Vee holds her hands up in front of her like they're a shield. "Hey, no judgment here. You do you."

"Seriously! Tell me why you laughed!"

Vee shrugs, all casual. "It's not your biggest fear."

"Oh, and you would know?"

Vee doesn't miss a beat. "Your biggest fear is you'll lose Shira."

My mouth falls open. "What's that supposed to mean?"

"Well, you've stared at her all through class for the last week. If you ask me, I'd say you're codependent."

"Coded-what?"

"You know." She cracks a smile. "Your self-worth is wrapped up in Shira, and for the first time in your life you're being asked to define yourself independently of her. That's terrifying for you."

I cross my arms over my chest. "Who do you think you are? Doctor Phil?"

Vee leans back in her chair and fiddles with that thing she keeps under her sweatshirt. I can see what it is now. It's the gold chain of a necklace. "My dad's a biopsychosocial psychologist," she says.

"Be that as it may," I say in my best I-know-what-a-bio-psycho-social-psychologist-is voice, "I'm not coded-whatever.

I'm afraid of spiders, and maybe heights, too, if you really want to know."

"Hey, I never said you weren't."

"Well, what are you afraid of then?"

"Forgetting my mom."

Just like that.

"Well that's . . ."

. . .

. . .

. . .

What *is* that?

Too serious?

Too honest?

Too much?

Too soon?

I don't know how you're supposed to respond to something like that. When someone is one hundred percent honest about something most people aren't usually honest about.

"She died when I was really little," says Vee. "And I already barely remember anything about her. Just little things from pictures, or stories. Oh, and the songs she used to play for me, I guess. But back when we were in Miami, living in a house that she lived in once, I felt like she was still kinda there, I guess. But now that we're here, I dunno. I can barely even play the flute in this new house . . ."

Her voice trails off, and I want to ask her more questions, but I don't want to seem nosy, and besides, Ms. Shapiro is flicking the lights on and off, so our conversation is officially over now.

But it's weird. This is the first discussion question all week—and maybe all year—where I wish I didn't have to stop.

After class, Shira and I walk to Spanish like we always do. "You and the new kid seem to be getting along," she says. "Kinda weird, huh?"

I stop walking. That's a strange question. And I'm not really sure how to respond.

I want to say we aren't "getting along" at all, that I'm convinced Vee doesn't like me very much.

I want to say I wouldn't have had to try to get along with Vee at all if *somebody* was still sitting next to me in social studies like they used to.

I want to say I'm not sure what or who she is referring to as "weird," because the only person around here who's been weird lately is her.

I do say, "Why do you care?"

Shira turns to look at me. "Because you were talking about me."

I knew we were being too loud!

"Why would we be talking about you?"

Shira raises her eyebrows, and I can't stop thinking about what Vee said about how my identity is defined by her. "That's what I want to know," Shira says.

"We weren't talking about you."

Shira nods, as if she doesn't quite believe me, and we start walking again, in silence. Like all the good feelings from this week—playing Boggle, having a sleepover, and our upcoming Shabbat dinner—are gone just like that.

"Whatever." Shira shakes her head. "You can talk to whoever you want, I guess."

She picks up her pace until she's two feet ahead of me, and by the time we get to class, it's like she's forgotten I was walking behind her. She goes straight to sit at a three-person desk pod with Sun and Angelica, leaving me to sit with Arya and Maria.

I think maybe Vee was right about my biggest fear.

The Final Straw

After school, Shira's not in our usual meet-up spot. Which is fine. She has math last period, and it probably ran over. Next week is Thanksgiving break, and all the teachers are assigning us extra homework.

But when I finally see her walking down the steps, she doesn't exactly seem to be rushing to meet me. She's dragging her feet and redoing her ponytail and adjusting her backpack straps, and when she finally does find me, she looks at the ground instead of at my eyes.

"Hey, Shira," I say. "Ready to go to your place for Shabbat?"

Instead of nodding and finding Grandma Mimi's car, she scrunches her nose. "Hannah?" She says it like a question, and that's when I know whatever is coming next is going to be bad. "I talked to my mom," she continues, "and she said I could take the bus to and from school."

"Oh." I swing my backpack off my shoulders. "Why would you want to do that?"

"Because I'm thirteen now. And my parents think it could be a good way for me to become more independent. It's probably easier for you too, since I'm always late in the mornings and my house isn't really on your way. And besides, Jeremy takes the bus, too, and—"

"Of course," I interrupt. "Jeremy Brewer."

Shira presses her lips together. "I knew you'd think this was about him."

"What else would it be about?"

"Oh, I dunno," Shira says. "Your fake bat mitzvah?"

"My . . . Wait—my *what?*"

"Hannah, please. Stop lying to me. Bat mitzvahs are, like, a really big thing. I know you're not preparing for one."

"But I *am* preparing for one." And I am. It's not a lie. "How would *you* know what I'm doing? I barely ever see you anymore."

"Okay, that's not fair. I'm sitting somewhere else in *one* class and we had a sleepover on Tuesday! Besides, I know you," she says. "I know you would rather spend your afternoons making the perfect apple pie than spend even a minute studying some religion you don't care about."

I can feel my blood pressure rising. "Who says I don't care about it?"

"Look, Hannah," Shira continues, "there's nothing wrong with not being Jewish! It's never mattered before that I am and you're not, so why are you pretending you *are* all of a sudden?"

Shira's face is soft, as if she's trying to be as nice and gentle as possible. She's not yelling at me. She's not angry.

But I'm angry enough for both of us.

"I *am* Jewish," I say. "You know that, right? I'm not pretending anything."

"Hannah, stop. It's honestly kind of insulting."

"*What* is insulting?! That I'm Jewish? How could that be insulting? It's who I am!"

"Fine. You're 'Jewish.'" She makes quotation marks with her fingers. "But you're not *really* Jewish. And that's fine!"

"But I am *really* Jewish."

"No, you're not! Not like I am, anyway. Or like Jeremy is. You've never tried to go to temple with me, you've never asked me about Hebrew school. I didn't even know you believed in God!"

"Oh, so I can't be Jewish if I don't go to temple? You know how my mom is. You know she wouldn't let me go even if I wanted to. And since when do you care if I believe in God or not?"

"That's what I'm saying, Hannah. I *don't* care what you believe in. And you've never cared about what I believe in, either. Up until now, anyway. It's like Jeremy was saying to me the other day. Jeremy said—"

"Ugh!" I shout. "Stop saying his name like that!"

"Like *what*?"

"Like you suddenly know him *so well* because you've been dating him for two seconds."

"He's my boyfriend, Hannah." Shira's voice is rising now.

"Only because you danced with him at your bat mitzvah instead of me like you promised."

"Promised?" Shira blows air out of her nose. "We talked about *maybe* dancing together *one time!* I never promised anything! You're just mad because Jeremy likes me and not you."

"I am *not!*" I shout. "This has nothing to *do* with that!"

"Then I have no idea why you're getting so mad." Shira puts her hands on her hips. "I'm trying to talk to you about something serious, and you're acting immature."

"Right, and you're *so* mature all of a sudden, now that you have a boyfriend. Look at you! You don't even need a ride to school anymore!"

My face is hot and tingly, and my throat is closing the way it does when I'm about to cry, and I don't want to cry in the middle of the lobby.

And now that I'm looking around, I'm noticing people watching me and Shira fight. Part of me is embarrassed, but another part wonders what they see when they look at us. Probably one beautiful girl with shiny hair and a brand-new boyfriend—a girl who was born knowing exactly who she was supposed to be—and one pathetic girl with gross braces and badly straightened hair, trying so hard to be something that maybe, when it comes down to it, she isn't.

"Do you even want to be my best friend anymore?" I ask, and I'm expecting her to stop me right there. To say *Of course I do!* and hug me and maybe tell me she didn't mean it about taking the bus to and from school. She'd miss me too much, and oh by the way, I am Jewish if I say I am, and let's go to Shabbat dinner right now and forget this ever happened.

But she doesn't say any of that. Instead she says, "Maybe we need a break from each other."

"A . . . a what?"

"You know, some time. To cool off."

"But I don't want to cool off."

"Yeah, well . . ." Shira looks at her feet. "I do."

I don't know what to say to that. I don't think there's anything *to* say.

"I'll see you after Thanksgiving." Shira waves and leaves. Probably to go meet *Jeremy*.

All I know is that I need to get out of there. Fast. So I throw myself against the lobby doors and find Grandma Mimi's car in the pickup queue, waiting, toasty warm. And Mrs. Rosen must have told her Shira isn't riding home with us today, or ever again, because she wraps her arms around me and says, "I know, bubbelah. I know," until I've cried myself out.

It's going to be a long winter.

Winter

Winter

Winter is when we make sufganiyot: jelly doughnuts, fried in oil.

"In honor of back to school!" Grandma Mimi says today as she stuffs a giant Tupperware container full of the winter treats into my backpack. "I'm giving you some extras," she says. "In case you need a peace offering."

"Hear, hear," I mumble.

I don't want to go back to school today. I want to keep watching TV just the way I did last week during Thanksgiving break. I want to sit in my pajamas and watch the powdered-sugar snow coat the sidewalk while I gorge myself on turkey and pumpkin pie. I want to hide in my house and pretend everything is normal. That Shira and I are fine, and the only reason we aren't talking right now is because she's busy with Thanksgiving.

But once I see her, I won't be able to pretend.

I try to get to school early so I can beat her to our usual pod with Delilah and Chris W., but Shira's already there by the time I arrive. When she sees me come in, she jerks her head away, as if the sight of me burns her eyes. And I guess that's it, then. Shira gets to sit with our friends in homeroom, and I'm stuck by myself.

At lunch, I don't bother going to the cafeteria. Shira doesn't want to sit with me, and I'm too sad to try to race her to the table, so I spend the period wandering the hallways until I find a room on the third floor that looks dark and empty.

At least I thought it was empty.

As soon as I flick the lights on, I hear a voice. "Maybe I had those off for a reason—ever think about that?"

I flick the lights back off. "Vee?"

"Good observation skills," she says.

"What are you doing here?"

Vee holds up the sandwich she's eating. "Perhaps I spoke too soon."

I open my mouth but shut it before I say anything else stupid.

"Are you going to eat your lunch with me?" Vee asks. "Or are you going to watch me eat from the doorway. Because you're welcome to watch, but I have to warn you, I charge a viewing fee."

I walk into the dark classroom and sit next to her. "Thanks," I say, pulling out my lunch and laying all the individual pieces on the table. A leftover Thanksgiving meal: turkey sandwich, cranberry sauce, caramelized carrots, pumpkin seeds, and a whole big tub of sufganiyot.

"Damn, you must be hungry," Vee says, nodding at the Tupperware, which I'm now realizing must have at least a dozen doughnuts stuffed inside it.

"Oh." I lift it up. "Heh. Yeah. It was supposed to be a peace offering for . . . well . . . I guess it doesn't matter now."

Vee taps her chin as if she's thinking, and says, "You are more than welcome to make peace with me."

"Help yourself." I hand her the open Tupperware. "They're my grandma's recipe. They're called—"

"I know what sufganiyot are," she says.

And just like that, she's surprised me again. "How do you know what they're called?"

Vee takes another bite. "Well, my family calls them buñuelos, but I've spent so much time in Ashkenazi-land that I've learned your native language."

My face must look as confused as I feel, because Vee rolls her eyes and pulls her necklace out of her shirt, the one she's always fiddling with. I've never been able to see what's on it, but now it's clear. It's the Star of David. Like Grandma Mimi's.

"You're not the only Jewish one around here," she says.

I must look like I swallowed a peach pit. "I . . . You . . . but you're Spanish!"

"Wow." Vee tucks the necklace back into her sweatshirt. "Just . . . wow. First off, I'm Guatemalan. Second, the two aren't mutually exclusive. And third, you have powdered sugar all over your chin."

I wipe the sugar—and my stupid look—off my face.

"You can apologize now," she says.

"Sorry."

"That was the worst apology I've ever heard."

"Sorry?"

Vee shakes her head. "Apologies have three parts. First, you have to know why what you said was wrong. Then you actually have to feel bad about it. Then you have to have a plan in place to never do it again."

I raise my eyebrows. This is the first I've heard about a recipe for an apology, and my face must look ridiculous, because Vee pats me on the shoulder. "It's okay. It takes a while to get the hang of apologizing. I'll temporarily forgive you, but, like, on probation. The next two hundred days in this icicle city are going to be long if I don't have anyone to eat lunch with."

"Thanks," I say, and I mean it. I really must be desperate for a friend, because having someone forgive me "on probation" is the best news I've had all day.

"You know, this apology lesson isn't free," Vee says, eyeing the nearly full Tupperware on my desk.

I laugh and give her one more sufganiyah, and one more when she finishes that one, and one more after that. And as the bell rings and Vee and I head to social studies, where we sit next to each other as though it's the most natural thing in the world, I realize something: this lunch period with Vee is the longest I've gone without feeling sad about Shira in a long time.

Sufganiyot

DRY yeast
    2T sugar + more for activation
    3/4C water ← *warm to the touch*
    2 1/2 C flour
    pinch of salt
    cinnamon to taste
    2 egg yolks
    2T butter

for filling:

jam, chocolate, cream

for dough:

Activate yeast. Mix dry ingredients, yolks, yeast, and knead.
Add butter, rise. ← OVERNIGHT
Cut dough circles and seal filling inside each with leftover egg
whites. Rise, and fry in hot oil until golden brown; fill, roll
in sugar, ~~cina~~cinnamon, or powdered sugar.

Remember:

Sufganiyot are best when they rise in the cold.

The colder the rise

the stronger the taste.

The Light

There's something weird that happens when you've been dumped by your best friend: suddenly you wish you had more homework.

Vee and I message online a bit when we get home from school, but she's a new friend, not a best friend, so our conversations are a bit short and stilted. If Shira were still speaking to me, I'd probably be at her place right now, sprawled on her bedroom floor, quizzing her on our Spanish vocab until we both got bored and switched to watching videos our friends post online.

But today Shira might be doing all that with Jeremy Brewer. Or Lin and Delilah. Or maybe by herself. And I'm sitting here trying to come up with any excuse I can to message Vee, because every time her three typing dots appear on my laptop screen, I feel a little less alone.

But eventually Vee needs to focus on her homework and eat dinner and help her brother study for his spelling test, and once she's signed off for good, I realize I'm all out of homework.

Well, except for studying my Torah portion.

I haven't looked at it in a week. Thanksgiving break was a good excuse not to do anything, since it's hard to practice singing when my parents aren't away at work all the time. But if

I'm being honest, at least part of the reason I've been putting it off is that I've had a mental block against it. Ever since my fight with Shira.

Whenever I pick up my packet, I hear her voice in my head. *You've never tried to go to temple with me. You've never asked me about Hebrew school. I didn't even know you believed in God!*

I know I have every right to study the Torah if I want to. No one can stop me from doing that. But Shira's not exactly wrong about what she said, either. I never tried to go to temple with her. I never asked her about Hebrew school. And I've never really thought much about whether or not I believe in God.

Maybe I don't deserve to study for a bat mitzvah.

But the longer I sit in my bedroom, the more bored I get and the more I think about my Torah portion.

And so, eventually, I practice.

I open my packet, set up the recording so I can listen to the first thirty seconds on repeat, and sink into the world of *Behar*.

But the weird thing is, as soon as I hit the play button, a wave of calm washes over me. Like I'm in my own world, separate from everything that hurts. I even try to sing along with the music a few times, but as hard as I try, it's nearly impossible to get my mouth to line up with the recording. The syllables stick in my throat, and the peaks and valleys of the melody fall flat on my tongue.

But I don't stop.

Every night this week I go to my room and practice. And as I practice, the song takes shape. The peaks and valleys feel intentional, not random, and the more I stare at the page, the more the letters make sense, too. The backwards *r*'s don't look so much like backwards *r*'s anymore. They look like a *kaf* here and a *vav* there, a *nun*, and then a *hei*. The backwards *c*'s don't look like backwards *c*'s either, and it makes me think about when I first started baking and I'd instead mix up salt and sugar, baking powder and baking soda, powdered sugar and cornstarch. Now it doesn't matter how similar the ingredients look. I know them inside and out, and the thought of mistaking one for the other is unimaginable.

I still don't know what it is I'm singing, because the English translation is difficult to decipher — something about farming laws? Honestly, it's kinda boring — but somehow, by Thursday after school, every sticky syllable finds its way into the hills and valleys of the chant.

It's not perfect, but it feels good. And sometimes it feels *great*. Sometimes I get that all-over tinginess again. That sugared syrup soaking into a pound cake feeling. That body-rocking, thigh-slapping, eyes-closing sort of music, and I know it's working.

Maybe I never tried to go to temple with Shira. And maybe

I never asked her about Hebrew school. And maybe I have no idea if I believe in God or not. But when I sing my Torah portion, I get this feeling that the words are part of me, and I'm part of them, and we're all part of something bigger than ourselves.

And when I feel that way, the only way to keep myself from bursting with it is to open my mouth and sing.

Leviticus 25:1–4

Vayedaber Adonay	God spoke
el-Moshe behar Sinay	to Moses at Mount Sinai
lemor.	saying
Daber el-beney Yisra'el	speak to the Israelites
ve'amarta alehem	and say to them
ki tavo'u	When you come into
el-ha'arets	the land
asher ani noten lachem	that I am giving you
v'shav'ta ha'arets	the land must be given
Shabat l'Adonay.	a Sabbath to God.
Shesh shanim	For six years
tizra sadecha	you may plant your fields
veshesh shanim	and for six years
tizmor	you may prune
karmecha	your vineyards
ve'asafta et-tevu'atah.	and harvest your crops.
Uvashanah hashvi'it	But the seventh year is a
Shabbat Shabbaton	Sabbath of Sabbaths
yihyeh la'arets	for the land.
Shabat l'Adonay	It is God's Sabbath
sadecha lo tizra	so do not plant your fields
vecharmecha lo tizmor.	or prune your vineyards.

Rote

When I sing for Aunt Yael on Thursday, I can tell I'm doing a good job. She smiles through the whole thing, correcting my pronunciation here and there, and when I'm done, she says, "Great job, Hannah! That was fantastic!"

And for a moment I'm thrilled. I did it! I *knew* I could do it, even if no one else thought I could. But I proved them wrong. I practiced hard, and Aunt Yael is actually happy with how I did. Maybe I really can do this, and in six months Shira will know that I wasn't lying about studying for my bat mitzvah and she'll *have* to be my best friend again.

"Now," Aunt Yael continues, pointing her finger at the page in front of me. "You sang the Hebrew well, but what does it mean?"

My smile disappears. "Umm . . . it's about God, or, rather, *Adonai,* and how, um, *Adonai* tells Moses that land—his land—needs a vacation?"

Aunt Yael smiles, laughs, throws her head back. "Ah!" she says. "You don't know anything until you know the *why.*"

My head falls forward onto the table. "Seriously?" I say. "I worked so hard! I studied every day for the past week, and I thought I was singing it right!"

"You did sing it right," she says. "Honestly, you sang it a whole lot better than I was expecting for your first real lesson. But that's exactly why it's time to move on to understanding it. Remember, being a bat mitzvah is about the *meaning* of the words, not just about reciting the Hebrew perfectly. Have you spent any time looking at the English translation?"

I quirk my mouth. "A little . . ."

"Is that a no?"

"No, I did. But it's kind of . . . hard to read."

Aunt Yael laughs once. "You mean boring."

I laugh right back. "Yeah," I say. "I do."

"Well, *Behar* is known for being a little . . ."

"Horrible?"

"I was going to say *dry,* but you'll find there's more to it than the obvious. The point of reading To-RAH "—emphasis on the RAH—"is choosing to look beneath the surface. When you become a bat mitz-VAH"—emphasis on the VAH—"you are transitioning from child to adult. A child would find *Behar* boring, but a bat mitz-VAH would see it as a metaphor for life. Because both life and the To-RAH are all about the *why*. So let's figure out your why. What is the thing that matters most to you?"

I don't even need to think about this one. "Food," I say, and I laugh like a puff of flour.

"Why is that funny?"

"It's not *funny* funny," I say. "It's . . . ridiculous funny. Isn't it? Food isn't important, it's just . . . food."

Aunt Yael props her chin on her palm. "How many times do we wash our hands during the Passover seder?"

"Huh?"

"You heard me. How many times do we wash our hands during the Passover seder?"

I shake my head.

"We wash our hands twice," she says. "Once before the rituals, and once before the meal. Do you know why that matters?"

I shake my head again.

"Because the meal is a ritual in and of itself. Bitter herbs represent the bitterness of slavery, an egg represents spring and the circle of life, salt water represents our tears, and that's not considering all the meaning a family creates when they eat the same food together year after year. There's nothing in the Torah about brisket, yet I've never hosted a Passover seder without one.

"And it's more than the food we eat, it's the rituals we discover along the way. Do you remember your cousins in San Francisco? The Adlers? I think their son Drake is about your age. Well, I remember how they always used to make this comment about how the Haggadah says we should *fill* our wineglasses, and we weren't following the rules unless they were full to the brim. When I was a kid, it drove me nuts when they said this, because they said it *every single year*. But now that I'm an adult, it doesn't feel like Passover unless someone says 'Full glasses!'"

Aunt Yael continues. "Of course, it's not only Passover that assigns meaning to food. On Yom Kippur we fast, on Rosh Hashanah we dip apples in honey, on Shabbat we gather not in front of a bema, but around the dinner table.

"We joke that Jewish holidays are all about the same thing: they tried to kill us, we survived, let's eat. And like all the best jokes, there's truth to it. Food is more than just food to us. It's a celebration. It's a religious practice. It's our culture, our family. It's a metaphor.

"Just like the Torah.

"Your homework for the week is to learn four more lines of your Torah portion, but it's not just that. I want you to spend the week figuring out how *Behar* can be a metaphor for your own life.

"*Behar* is about giving the land a sabbatical year. A rest. It's about how we can't take it for granted, or it will stop giving us what we need. So I want you to think about the ecosystems in our life that might need a sabbatical year. What might improve if given a rest? What relationships need time to recover? When should we pause and take a breath instead of rush, rush, rush? When should we take a moment to ... digest?" Aunt Yael smiles. "Pun intended."

I nod. I think I can do that.

"And Hannah," she adds. "Whatever you do, don't rule out food. If food is important to you, that doesn't make you ridiculous.

"What that makes you is—Jewish."

The Fight

I think about food on the way home from Aunt Yael's. How my family will take the excuse of any birthday, holiday, or just plain Wednesday to craft a masterpiece out of flour and butter and sugar. How, at almost any hour of the day, my kitchen smells like heaven. How, no matter what's going on in our lives, my family stops what we're doing at dinnertime to sit around the table and eat Grandma Mimi's cooking.

Maybe Aunt Yael was right, and food isn't ridiculous at all. Maybe it is a metaphor, a culture, a celebration. The glue that fills the cracks in my family and keeps us from completely coming apart.

But if that's true, why do Dad and Sam keep fighting about it?

When we get home, they're going at it in the living room. And from the sound of it, it's been going on for a while.

"Don't think you're going to be able to accept their offer!" Dad shouts.

"Do you realize what an honor it is to get in?" Sam shouts back.

Mom's sitting at the kitchen table with her laptop open in front of her, head in her hands, while her son and husband fight in the next room.

"What?" Grandma Mimi says as we walk inside. "I'm gone for two hours and you can't keep them apart?"

Mom shakes her head. "It's bad this time. Sam got into culinary school, and he insists that he's going. I've tried to break them up, but it's like they can't hear me. I don't know what to do."

Grandma Mimi and I share a look, but then she waggles her eyebrows. "Sounds like it's time I brought in backup."

She opens the freezer, digs around for a few minutes, and, from the no man's land of the bottom shelf, unearths an entire blood orange pie in mint condition.

"How did that get there?" I ask.

"What?" Grandma Mimi says, like she's all offended. "You don't think I have a pie for every problem?" She winks at me and heats up two slices.

The two voices grow louder in the next room.

"I don't care if it's an honor. You're not going!"

"I don't think you get a say in where I go to college!"

"Hey," Grandma Mimi shouts, entering the room with a big, booming stomp.

But Dad and Sam barely seem to notice.

"I have a say in where you go to college as long as I'm paying for it!"

"Well, maybe I don't need you to pay for it!"

"Hey!" Grandma Mimi shouts again, stomping her heel on the wooden floor.

But Dad and Sam continue their fight without so much as a glance in our direction.

"Oh yeah, I'd love to see how you manage that!"

"Fine! If this is about money, I can make it about money! Not every job requires an M.B.A. I have ways of making money you couldn't even imagine!"

"HEY!" Grandma Mimi drops the plates on the coffee table in front of them with such a loud *clang* that finally, they look up.

"Eat some pie, eh?" Grandma Mimi says now that she has their attention. "I'll go make dinner."

Everything is quiet then, except for the sounds of chewing and forks clinking on plates, with an "Oh, this is so good" thrown in now and again.

The quiet lasts through the night. Dinner, dessert, homework, but this is the first time I've seen Grandma Mimi have so much trouble breaking up one of Dad and Sam's fights.

She's never had to shout more than once or twice to get their attention, and I'm not sure I like how hard it was for her to stop this one.

I guess it's like when you punch down a ball of bread dough after the first rise. You're not killing the yeast, you're just popping the bubbles. This fight is far from over, and it's going to get worse before it gets better.

The silence is dense that night. Thick and obvious, as if everyone is walking on eggshells. "What if they never make up?" I ask Grandma Mimi as she tucks me into bed. "The fighting keeps getting worse and worse. What happens when they decide it's not worth making up anymore?" I picture Mom and Aunt Yael in my head, and then the image is immediately replaced by me and Shira, Dad and Sam. What if all these fights aren't temporary? What if they go on and on, and seven years from now, Shira still won't speak to me, and Dad and Sam can't be in the same room together?

Grandma Mimi sits on the edge of my bed. "You know, I hate it when they fight, but sometimes even the best relationships need a break. We just need a little patience and a little trust in the strength of their bond. Maybe if they rush this fight, they'll miss out on an opportunity to grow. To change. To evolve. And if they give themselves some time to rest, maybe they'll come back stronger than ever."

Something about what she's saying sounds familiar, but I can't put my finger on it.

"And anyway," Grandma Mimi says, "I have a plan. Don't you worry about it."

It makes me feel better that Grandma Mimi has a plan, that at least someone has a handle on things, so I say good night, and as I'm drifting off to sleep, I think about Dad and Sam. I think about me and Shira. I think about Mom and Aunt Yael, and I try to tell myself the fights are part of it all. Part of being a friend, part of being a family. Maybe fighting is one of the ingredients of a relationship. And maybe we don't like it any more than we like to wait around for our bread to rise, but maybe the waiting is as important as the eating.

It's only after I'm finally drifting off to sleep that I realize it's barely four hours after my lesson with Aunt Yael and I already understand *Behar* a whole lot better than I did this morning.

Recipe for My New Life

Mix together
    quiet on the ride to school
        even though Grandma Mimi tries
        to liven it up
        with KISS FM
        instead of her boring classical station,
    quiet on the ride from school
        even though Grandma Mimi tries
        to liven it up
        by asking me questions
        about my day,
    lunch in the third-floor classroom
        in the dark
        with a girl who wears ripped-up jeans
        and says words like *codependent,*
    and way too much time
        spent in my bedroom
        practicing my Torah portion.

Leviticus 25:5-7

Et sefiach ketsircha

Do not harvest the crops
that grow on their own

lo tiktsor ve'et-inevey

do not gather the grapes

nezirecha lo tivtsor

on your unpruned vines

shnat Shabbaton

since it is a year of rest

yihyeh la'arets.

for the land.

Vehayetah Shabat ha'arets

What grows while
the land rests

lachem le'ochlah lecha

may be eaten by you

ule'avdecha vela'amatecha

your servants

velischricha

and the employees

uletoshavecha hagarim imach

who live with you.

Velivhemtech velachayah

All the crops shall be eaten

asher be'artsecha tihyeh

by the domestic and wild

chol tevu'atah le'echol.

animals that are in
your land.

The Best Relationships

At my next lesson, while Aunt Yael prepares biscuits and jelly, I explain my brainstorm about the *why* of *Behar*.

"So the land would be Dad and Sam," I say, "or me and Shira. And we need a rest. Like, our relationships do. And if we push through, it could be bad in the long run. But if we take a break, things will be better off down the road."

"Exactly!" Aunt Yael brings over the platter of biscuits. "What I love about this portion is it reminds me that nothing exists solely for our benefit. In *Behar,* God tells Moses the land belongs to God—but to me, the land represents any living ecosystem."

"Yeah." I take a biscuit from the plate and slather it with jelly. "That's what I was getting at."

"Whenever we find ourselves clinging too hard to something, it's important to remember it exists outside of our need for it. That goes for our relationships with our communities, our friends, our family members. These relationships are all living organisms, separate from us, which means they don't belong to us, but rather to God.

"We tend them and prune them and harvest them, but even the best relationships sometimes need a sabbatical year."

I nod and take a bite of my biscuit. "Yeah," I say. "A sabbatical—" But as soon as the taste of the jelly hits my tongue, I stop speaking.

It tastes familiar.

It's sweet. No—spicy. No—sweet and spicy.

I've had this jelly before.

I close my eyes to remember when, and all of a sudden it's like I'm five years old again. On a picnic with my family—me, Sam, Mom, Dad, Grandma Mimi, Grandpa Joseph, and Aunt Yael—eating beer-battered chicken, blue cheese mashed potatoes, and buttermilk biscuits topped with this exact jelly.

"Is this . . ." I lick the remnants off my lips. "Is this spicy watermelon jelly?"

Aunt Yael smiles. "I was wondering if you'd remember."

I scoop a bit of jelly onto my finger and stick it into my mouth, savoring the spicy-sweet taste on my tongue. "I haven't had Grandma Mimi's watermelon jelly in ages."

"That's because it's not her recipe." Aunt Yael rips off a piece of biscuit and stares at it. "It was mine. Well—" Aunt Yael pauses. "Mine and your mom's."

That's when I realize this whole conversation, about fighting and forgiveness and sabbatical years, was never just about Sam and Dad fighting over culinary school or me and Shira fighting over bat mitzvahs.

Aunt Yael puts the biscuit back on her plate. "Your mom still hasn't told you what happened between us, has she."

She doesn't say it like a question, but I nod anyway. "Could you tell me what happened?"

I hold my breath so as not to break the spell. This is finally it. The time has come. Today, in Aunt Yael's kitchen, I'm going to get answers.

But when Aunt Yael speaks, she doesn't answer my question. Instead she says, "Do you know what *tikkun olam* means?"

I shake my head.

"It means 'to heal the earth.' I think about it a lot because it reminds me that although there is bad in the world, it's our job as Jews, and as humans, to repair it.

"So often, we talk about *tikkun olam* when we are the ones who are hurt. When something horrible happens in the world, something out of our control, we feel powerless. When we are persecuted, victimized, oppressed, when hatred rears its head, it is easy to feel like the world is too much to bear. But there is tremendous power in turning our own hurting into healing. Into *tikkun olam*. It helps to focus our feelings of helplessness into action. We can't heal the earth by ourselves, but if we all live in the spirit of *tikkun olam,* in the long run, the earth will be healed.

"But *tikkun olam* isn't just for when we're hurt. It's also for when we're the ones who cause the hurt. *Tikkun olam* is about atoning. About healing the hurt we caused. And of course, no one owes anybody forgiveness, but our hope is that our lives will heal more cracks in the earth than they create.

"I tell you this because as much as I want to give you my side of the story about what happened between me and your mother, I think that would cause her more hurting than healing. But if your mother does choose to tell you and you still want to hear my side, I'd be happy to share it."

Buttermilk Biscuits

4C flour

1/2C powdered buttermilk — NOT LIQUID!!!!!

sugar to taste

1t baking soda

4t baking powder

BIG ^ pinch of salt

1 1/2 sticks butter ← (melts in the oven, melts in your mouth!)

4T ~~vegtable~~ vegetable shortening

1 1/2C whole milk.

Mix dry ingredients, add chilled butter + shortening. Mix. Add milk. Mix. Knead the dough and roll into a tube. Cut biscuits and bake at 450 degrees until golden brown.*

*Can reduce to 400 degrees after 5 minutes for softer center.

Remember:

Steer clear of the kitchen while they're in the oven.

Biscuits don't brown if you're ~~spying~~ on them!

Watermelon Jelly

Grandma Mimi makes honey chili chicken for dinner tonight, but I must be sleepy, and when I'm sleepy, sometimes I say things I shouldn't. "You know what I just remembered?" I say. "I haven't thought of it in years, but I remembered how I used to love watermelon jelly."

Mom's fork drops to the floor.

"Whoops." She picks it up. "Sorry. Why were you thinking about watermelon jelly?"

I'm not sure what I was hoping would happen. I guess I thought if I asked about Aunt Yael without actually asking about her, I'd trick Mom into telling me something important. Something that could help me figure out what happened between them.

"Oh, you know," I say, pushing further than I probably should. "Spicy-sweet chicken, spicy-sweet jelly. We should make it again sometime!"

Mom pushes her mouth into a smile and says, "Sure. Anytime."

Recipe for Family Secrets Strudel

Mix together
butter and flour
salt and water
to get a rough dough
that pulls away from any sort of contact
with the sides of the bowl.
Turn the dough onto a lightly floured surface
and knead and push and knead and push
until it resembles a square
that you will refrigerate until it's nice and
cold.
When it's done chilling
take your butter and flatten it out
in the middle of your rolled-out dough
before folding it inside
like a letter
you don't want anyone to read.
Rotate, refrigerate, and repeat
six times
—no!
twelve times
—no!

twenty-four times
—no!
infinity plus one times.
Layers and layers and layers
and layers and layers and layers
of secrets.
Let it chill overnight
or over seven years
so all the ingredients are cold and
unmoldable.
Stuck in their forms
and unwilling to soften.
Then
and only then
can you add the apples
sweetened with brown sugar
and sprinkled with raisins
so even after you've folded your strudel
and baked it to a crisp
you're still finding tiny bits of secret
raisins
for years
and years
to come.

Pescacide

"Maybe your aunt killed your mom's fish," says Vee the next day during social studies.

The question of the day was something about what piece of art you would want to hang in your bedroom if given the opportunity, but somehow the question spiraled, and now we're talking about . . .

"Pescacide," Vee says. "The most unforgivable of crimes."

I have to laugh at that, and when I do, I realize this might be the first time I've laughed—*really* laughed—since my fight with Shira.

"Or maybe," Vee continues, "your aunt stole your mom's favorite hair tie. That's grounds for excommunication in our house."

I laugh again, full on in my belly this time. "It's gotta be the hair tie thing," I say. "Definitely, one hundred percent, the hair tie thing."

"I dunno," says Vee. "Pescacide is a serious crime! My money is on the fish."

She makes a face like she's a dead fish, and it's so stupid-looking that I let out a screech-laugh so loud that Shira glances at me from across the room.

Maybe she misses me.

Maybe she wishes she knew what I was laughing about.

Maybe she remembers how much *we* used to laugh together.

"I just want to do something," I say, tearing my eyes away from Shira. "Like, if I knew what happened between Mom and Aunt Yael, maybe I could help them make up."

I'm not sure where this statement comes from, but as soon as I say it, I know it's true. I *would* like to help Mom and Aunt Yael make up. I feel like even Grandma Mimi wants me to help them make up. She did mention something about forgiveness when I first asked her about visiting Aunt Yael. Maybe she thinks I can be a peace offering between them.

I look over at Shira once more, and now she's the one laughing without me. My ex–best friend and her boyfriend, giggling about who-knows-what, and as much as I like my new friend, I sure do miss my old one.

My life might be a funhouse mirror version of what it once was, but just because I can't heal the cracks in *my* earth doesn't mean I can't try to heal the cracks in someone else's.

Leviticus 25:8–9

Vesafarta lecha sheva
shabtot shanim sheva
shanim sheva pe'amim
vehayu lecha yemey
sheva shabtot hashanim
tesha ve'arba'im shanah.
Veha'avarta shofar tru'ah
bachodesh hashvi'i
be'asor lachodesh
beYom haKippurim
ta'aviru shofar
bechol-artsechem.

You shall count seven
sabbatical years, that is,
seven times seven years.
The period of the seven
sabbatical cycles shall thus
be forty-nine years.
Then, on the tenth day of
the seventh month, you
shall make a proclamation
with the ram's horn.
This proclamation is thus to
be made on Yom Kippur.

Forgiveness

Tikkun olam.

That's what Aunt Yael called it.

The attempt to heal the earth.

When she mentioned it in our lesson last week, I thought I'd never heard of it before. But as I read the next few lines in my Torah portion, I realize maybe I have.

This proclamation is thus to be made on Yom Kippur.

See, I've heard of Yom Kippur. Every fall, Grandma Mimi celebrates it. Although I'm not sure if Yom Kippur is something you can "celebrate," since it involves not eating for a whole day, but whatever. She recognizes it, anyway. And as I was practicing my Torah portion this week, I remembered that one year I asked Mom if I could go to temple with Grandma Mimi. Well, I think that holiday was Yom Kippur. See, when we were in the car, before I fell asleep, I remember Grandma Mimi talking about how it was the Day of Atonement. We don't eat, because we want to remove all distractions and focus on the purpose of the day: atoning for our sins.

Today I looked it up, and atoning doesn't mean just feeling bad about your sins. It doesn't mean saying you're sorry for them and forgetting they ever happened. That's like covering up a crack in a cheesecake by adding raspberries. It doesn't actually fix the problem, it simply makes the problem harder to see.

No. Atoning is apologizing, which means it has a recipe.

It means knowing why what you did was wrong. It means apologizing, and *meaning* it. It means fixing the damage you caused and making sure it never happens again.

Well, maybe if Mom knew the apology recipe, she could make up with Aunt Yael.

I knock on the door to her office. "Mom?"

"Oh! Hannah!" she says. "What's going on? You never come into my office!"

She pulls her reading glasses up onto her head while she looks at me, and something about how she does this reminds me of Aunt Yael. Maybe it's a sign that today is the day they finally atone. Maybe that means I'm on the right track trying to bring them back together.

"I've been wanting to talk to you about something for a while," I say, pulling up the extra chair so it's facing her. "I know I've asked you this before, but I've been thinking about it, and maybe I can help. If you'll talk to me, that is.

"So I wanted to know.

"What actually happened between you and Aunt Yael?"

Recipe for Catching My Mother Off-Guard

Mix together
one (1) mouth in the shape of an O
    like the hole inside
    of a bundt cake
ten (10) fingers
    interlaced
    so they almost look like they're
    praying
three (3) throat-clearing coughs
    che-che-chem!
one (1) hair
    smooth-down
and finally
one (1) nonanswer:

"Hannah, it's sweet that you want to help. Really, it is. But there's truly nothing you can do to fix this problem.

"Your Aunt Yael betrayed me. Remember how I said religion can be bad? Well, she's living proof of that. She's not a good person, and that's all you need to know.

"End of discussion."

Betrayal

I can't picture it.
I can't picture Aunt Yael betraying anybody.
I can't picture this woman—
who takes me in
   on Thursday afternoons
who bakes rugelach
   like Grandma Mimi
who slaps her hands on her thighs
   while she sings
who is the only person
   other than my grandmother
   who seems to think I'm Jewish—
ever betraying anyone.

And all through our next lesson
the one right before our big winter break
I find myself staring at her
wondering
wondering
wondering . . .

. . . what on earth happened between them?

Leviticus 25:10–14

Vekidashtem et shnat hachamishim shanah ukratem dror ba'arets lechol-yoshveyha yovel hi tihyeh lachem veshavtem ish el-achuzato ve'ish el-mishpachto tashuvu.

You shall sanctify the fiftieth year, declaring emancipation of slaves all over the world. This is your jubilee year when each man shall return to his home and family.

Yovel hi shnat hachamishim shanah tihyeh lachem lo tizra'u velo tiktseru et-seficheyha velo tivtseru et-nezireyha.

The fiftieth year shall also be a jubilee to you as you may not sow, harvest growing crops, nor gather grapes.

Ki yovel hi kodesh tihyeh lachem min-hasadeh tochlu et-tevu'atah.

The jubilee will be holy. You shall eat the crops from the field that year.

Bishnat hayovel hazot tashuvu ish el-achuzato.

In the jubilee year every man will return to his hereditary property.

Vechi timkeru mimkar la'amitecha o kanoh miyad amitecha al-tonu ish et-achiv.

Thus, when you buy or sell land to your neighbor, do not cheat each other.

Jubilee

I'd never tell Grandma Mimi this, but Christmas is my favorite holiday.

There's no school, and the house always smells like roasting meat, fried dough, and pine needles. Plus, I love having two whole weeks where I have to do nothing except hoard blankets to protect against the cold that leaks in through our drafty windows.

I love watching the presents pile up under the Christmas tree as the days march forward to December 25, and I love how we're allowed to open just one present on Christmas Eve, and I love it when Grandma Mimi tries to convince Mom to let me and Sam light the Hanukkah candles with her. Mom always says no, but at this time of year, even fights about Hanukkah feel like a celebration.

Or a jubilee, as my Torah portion would call it.

"Hannah?" Dad stumbles up the stairs from the basement, carrying a giant, dusty box. It's the first Monday of winter break, so it's officially tree-decorating day. "Sam?" Dad sets down the box of ornaments. "Who wants to help decorate the tree?"

I'm playing *Zelda* on our TV, curled up beneath a big, squishy blanket, and Sam is lying on the couch in sweatpants, reading some fat book with a picture of outer space on the cover. Only now do I realize it's the first time I've seen Sam in the house since his big fight with Dad. He's been waking up early and coming home late. Maybe he's avoiding us.

But today Sam's actually here. Downstairs, mostly awake, and to my surprise, when Dad starts untangling Christmas lights, Sam doesn't grumble about Hallmark holidays and consumer culture. He puts down his book and helps.

It's a Christmas miracle!

"Who wants pancakes?" Grandma Mimi asks.

"Me!" I say.

"Chocolate chip?" Sam asks.

"Of course," Grandma Mimi replies. "What do you think this is, amateur hour?"

"Me too," says Mom, coming down the stairs in her robe and flannels.

"Who has time to eat?" Dad asks, waving a string of lights in the air. "We have work to do!"

Grandma Mimi pats Dad on his cheek and says "Mishigas" before heading back into the kitchen.

"All right, Sam." Dad hands Sam the lights. "You help me untangle this one, and Hannah, you go through those light bulbs and figure out which one's the dud."

"You know," says Sam, "they make lights now that don't all crap out when one bulb dies."

Dad laughs. "Where's the fun in that?"

Grandma Mimi comes back in from the kitchen. "Are we out of flour?" she asks.

Sam drops the string of lights he's holding.

"I could have sworn I just bought some," Grandma Mimi continues. "A big sack of it, last week at the store."

"Oh," says Sam. "That might have been the cupcakes I made for Zach Stone's birthday on Thursday."

"I thought Zach Stone's birthday was in August," I say.

Sam shoots me a look, and I shut my mouth with a snap.

"Sorry, not Zach Stone," he says. "Zach Carter."

"Oh, right," I say, even though I'm pretty sure Sam went to a birthday party for Zach Carter this past summer too.

"Huh," grunts Dad. "You'd think someone who wants to be a pastry chef would know how to buy more flour when he uses the last of it."

All of a sudden the cozy Christmas air turns cold and drafty again.

"Oh!" Grandma Mimi says. "I forgot! I spilled the flour while I was making sufganiyot. I must have forgotten to add it to the list. Oy vey!"

Dad makes a sound like he's not quite sure if he believes her, and I make a big show about asking her to pick me up some oranges while she's at the store.

But there's something about Christmas that turns the sourest mood into one that tastes like bright, citrusy chocolate, because soon Dad's humming along to some jingly song playing on the speakers, Grandma Mimi's back home with a trunkful of flour and oranges, Mom's asking how we want our bacon, and after nearly thirty minutes of replacing light bulbs one by one, my whole string lights up.

Chocolate Chocolate Chip Pancakes

1 1/2 C flour

1/4 C cocoa powder

2T sugar ⟵ + 2T brown sugar!

2t baking powder

pinch of salt

1t ~~vanilla~~ vanilla extract

cinnamon to taste

1 1/2C buttermilk

2 eggs

3T butter

~~choclate~~ chocolate chips to taste

Whisk dry ingredients in one bowl, wet in the other. Slowly whisk wet ingredients into dry. Add chocolate chips and cook in a hot buttered skillet until bubbles form. Flip and serve.

DO NOT overmix

Remember:

Don't fight the lumps in the pancake batter.

It's what makes them nice and fluffy.

Recipe for Christmas Dinner

Mix

one (1) brisket

one (1) tray of balsamic Brussel sprouts

seventy-nine (79) potato latkes

   (we might have gone overboard)

one (1) tub of cinnamon-strawberry applesauce

one (1) tub of fresh sour cream

one (1) chocolate cake

two (2) chicken-wing oven mitts

   that were one of my Christmas gifts

one (1) Christmas tree

   twinkling away in our living room

one (1) happy family

   making Christmas dinner

   together.

The Gift

By the time Christmas is over, everyone's exhausted from opening presents and stuffed to the brim from eating too much. Mom and Dad go to bed early, since Dad needs to get up for work in the morning, and Grandma Mimi can't keep her eyes open late enough to get through a Christmas movie marathon. Sam went out again, as soon as the last of the presents were opened, which is weird. Who would he be seeing on Christmas?

That's why, when I hear a knock on my bedroom door, I assume I've imagined it.

It's quiet, as if whoever it is doesn't want to wake anybody else, so when I go to answer it, I tiptoe.

And standing at the door, her right hand hidden behind her back, is Grandma Mimi. "Shh," she whispers. "Can I come in? I have a present for you."

I move aside so she can come past me. "Didn't I already open all my Christmas presents?"

Grandma Mimi pulls her hand out from behind her back, revealing a small, delicately wrapped package. "Then consider this a Hanukkah present."

I take the box from her and slowly tear off the wrapping paper, savoring the sound it makes as it rips, until I see one of those black velvet boxes you find on commercials for diamond rings. But inside the box isn't a diamond ring, it's a tarnished silver star at the end of a finely linked chain.

"Wow," I say, taking it out of its box. "This is just like yours."

Grandma Mimi clutches her own silver star at the nape of her neck. "It was your mother's. Or at least I wanted it to be. I gave it to her for her bat mitzvah, just like I did for your Aunt Yael. But your mother never wanted to wear it. Even before everything happened, she was never a necklace sort of person. I knew that, but until I moved into this house, I'd assumed she always kept it somewhere safe. Special.

"Until one day when I decided to clean out the attic. Halfway through schlepping boxes up and down the stairs, I found it.

"She hadn't been keeping it anywhere special at all.

"She put it into storage, like it was dreck.

"And that's her decision. I don't hold it against her, but I wish things had gone differently.

"So, here, Hannah. It's yours now.

"I know I promised I would talk to your mother about you seeing your Aunt Yael, and I will. I swear I will. But I wanted you to have this now, so you never question that you are Jewish. If I tell your mother and she throws a fit? Feh! Doesn't change a thing, because you, my Hannah, are Jewish."

She kisses me on the forehead, and before making her way

out the door, she adds one final point. "Maybe keep the necklace in its box until I do have a chance to talk to your mother, eh? She might not love you wearing it."

And with that, she's gone.

Engraving

I put on the necklace, just for the night, and fall asleep.

When I wake up, I take it off and put it in my pocket before Mom can see. But when I look in the mirror, I notice a small six-pointed star imprinted right in the middle of my chest.

Happy New Year!

Every New Year's Eve, Shira's family hosts a party. It's usually fun, and they hire fancy caterers who make a chocolate torte I can't reproduce no matter how much I try.

And trust me, I've tried.

There are about a billion people there. Her parents invite everyone they know, and all her cousins are in town because it's winter break. The best part is, her two Virginia cousins always bring these Great Danes named Vim and Vigor, and we all chase them around the playroom until they knock something over and Shira's dad comes down to tell us to stop tormenting the poor dogs.

This year, Vim and Vigor will have one fewer tormentor. Even though Shira hasn't said anything to me explicitly, I know she doesn't want me there tonight.

"Hannah?" Mom finds me in the living room, sitting on the couch with Sam, watching our sixth episode of *Queer Eye*. "Will you be ready to go to the Rosens' soon?"

"No," I say. "I'm not going." I try to keep my voice calm, try not to think about how badly I want to be at that party. Try not to remember how Shira and I always stay up practically until sunrise playing *Settlers of Catan*, and how last year I laughed so hard at one point I almost peed my pants.

I don't need a big party. This year, I'm ringing in the new year with the Fab Five.

"Get up," Mom says, as if she didn't hear me. "Get showered, get dressed, and put on a nice dress. We're leaving soon."

"No," I say louder. "Shira doesn't want me there."

Mom takes the remote from the coffee table and shuts off the TV.

"Hey!" Sam says. "Can't you two discuss this somewhere else?"

Mom ignores Sam. "Hannah, why do you think Shira doesn't want you there?"

"Because she doesn't," I say. "Shira hates me."

"Shira doesn't *hate* you. You're her best friend! You're having a fight."

"It's not a regular fight," I say. And it's *not* a regular fight. This is more like a sabbatical year.

"Mom, let her do what she wants," Sam butts in. "Why can't she stay here?"

"Yeah!" I say. "I'll stay here with Sam!"

"Well," Mom says. "Sam's going to Amit's house in a little bit. Do you want to go to Amit's house too?"

"Oh no," Sam says. "She's not coming with me!"

"Ew, I don't want to go to your friend's house anyway."

"So, what?" Mom asks. "You'll sit here all night?"

"I guess." I say. "Better than being somewhere where everyone hates me."

Mom rubs her forehead with her fingertips. "This fight is getting ridiculous, Hannah. I'm sure if you talked to Shira, things would go right back to normal."

"I've tried talking to her," I say. "She doesn't want anything to do with me."

Mom takes a deep breath and sits on the couch beside me, throwing her arm around my shoulders, as if hugging me will magically make Shira want to be my friend again. "I think your relationship is stronger than this fight," Mom says. "You've spent so many happy years together, and I'm sure she wants to make up with you just as much as you want to make up with her."

Maybe I'm just trying to change the subject. Maybe I hate the thought of my parents and Grandma Mimi going to Shira's house, pretending everything is normal, when I'm at home watching TV in my pajamas.

But Mom's words give me an idea, and I can't pass it up. So I squeeze the necklace that now sits in my left-side pajama pants pocket, and I say, "You know what? You might be right, Mom."

"I might?" She seems skeptical.

"Yeah. What if I go to Shira's tonight and try one more time to make up with her—but you need to call Aunt Yael before we leave and do the same."

Sam looks at me, impressed, but Mom doesn't seem very happy. "That's an entirely different situation."

"I'm not sure if it is," I say. "Because you're right. Friendship should be strong enough to withstand one fight. But sisterhood should be even stronger. If you try, I'll try."

Mom takes a deep breath and kneads her forehead before standing up and leaving the room. It all happens so fast, I'm not entirely sure what the resolution in our argument was, but a few minutes later I hear Mom tell Dad, "Hannah's not coming. Let's get going."

I click *Queer Eye* back on and nestle into my blankets. I guess I won, though it doesn't quite feel like a victory.

Forget the chocolate torte. Tonight I'm making myself feel better with baklava.

Baklava

1 package ~~philo~~ phyllo dough ←

1 lb nuts (walnuts for smokiness, pistachios for oiliness)

2 sticks butter

1t cinnamon

1C water

1C sugar

1t vanilla

1/2C honey

Chop nuts, toss with cinnamon, and cut dough to fit in pan.

Layer dough, butter, nuts, like this:

dough
butter →
nuts →

Cut into triangles and bake at 350 until crisp and golden.

When it's done, spoon simmered sugar, water, vanilla, honey mixture onto baklava.

Do this IMMEDIATELY after baking!!!

Remember:

For therapeutic baklava: crush nuts with a hammer.

For less mess: use a food processor.

Countdown

Ten
nine
eight
seven
six
five
four
three
two
one

happy new year to me
and baklava for sixteen
for one.

Back to School

Back-to-school Monday is a marble swirl of a day, with everyone except Dad and Sam forgetting to set their alarms and waking up in a panic when the garbage trucks beep outside our front yard.

With my rude awakening, I have fifteen minutes to straighten my hair and put my new necklace in my pocket before we're out the door and I'm nodding off in the passenger seat of Grandma Mimi's car. She must be half asleep too, because I wake up to her making a U-turn and mumbling something under her breath.

"Whoops. Old habits . . ." she says, and I blink my eyes open to realize we're pulling away from Shira's house. "Sorry, bubbelah," Grandma Mimi says. "Took the old turn by mistake. Back on our way to school."

And as we drive back the way we came, I look through our rear window to see Shira leaving her house. She doesn't seem to notice our car, which is good, I guess, but it's weird. I think this winter break is the longest I've gone without seeing her since we met.

She must have gotten a haircut recently, since it's shorter than I remember, and I don't recognize the jacket she's wearing—must have been a Hanukkah present—and I think her boots might be new too. It's like every day I don't see her, she changes a little bit, and as those little changes add up, she becomes more and more a stranger to me.

Before I know it, school has begun, and I'm sitting in social studies with Vee, and except for the purple streak in her hair that's magically turned blue, she looks the same as ever.

"Hi," I say.

"Salutations," she says back, and with that, it's like no time has passed. We dive into our first partner discussion question of the new year, "What I Did Over My Winter Break," but it isn't long before our conversation shifts away from sleeping late and boring TV binges to more interesting things, like baklava and sufganiyot.

Before long, Vee is asking me if I want to go to her house tomorrow night to bake with her. "My Tía Rosa is in town," she says, "and she wants to teach me how to make buñuelos. You know, like sufganiyot, but better. I feel like you would be an asset in the kitchen, so wanna join?"

She's fiddling with her necklace as she asks me this, the way she always does when she's nervous or uncomfortable, but this time, I have a twin necklace in my pocket, which I squeeze too. "I'd love to come!" I say. "Can't wait!"

And I mean it. This is a fresh year and a fresh start. And there's nothing I'd love to do more than start it off with my new friend, Vee.

Recipe for Back to School Snickerdoodles

Cream together
butter and shortening
but add some rainbow sprinkles into the mix
so it's bright and cheerful.

Mix in the white sugar
and the eggs
but spring for the fresh ones this time
with the bright yellow yolks
from the Saturday morning farmers' market
so it tastes like blue skies in winter.

Blend in the all-purpose flour,
cream of tartar, salt
and don't forget the baking soda too
so it rises up big and fluffy.

Roll them into balls
and sprinkle cinnamon on them
—no
cinnamon sugar
—no

cinnamon sugar with dribbles of caramel
and chocolate sauce
because why not!

School has started again
and I'm going to Vee's house tomorrow
and I can feel it in my bones:
it's going to be a great year.

A Great Year

The next day, Vee's dad picks us up after school. "The famous Hannah!" he says, turning down the radio so we can hear each other talk. Vee's dad looks exactly how I pictured him. Short, like Vee, dark skin, like Vee, and dark hair, like Vee, except without a blue streak. "I'm Raúl," he continues. "And I hope you're hungry. I don't know what Victoria has told you about buñuelos, but after tonight, you'll wish you had two stomachs."

We drive away from school, in the same direction Grandma Mimi always drives when we go home. I keep waiting for us to make an unfamiliar turn or a weird exit, but it never happens, and before long, we turn into the driveway of the house with the yellow door.

"Hey, wait a second," I say. "I know this house! We drive past here every day! I live just a few blocks down."

Vee's dad holds out his gloved hand for a high-five and says, "Neighbors!"

I stare at it, not sure if I'm supposed to slap it or not. I don't think I've given someone a non-ironic high-five since kindergarten. Vee pulls his hand to his side and says, "Dad, no." Then, to me, "You don't need to humor him," and I laugh because sometimes it feels like Vee and I share the same brain.

We seem to share the same house, too. Hers is also one of those old types of houses, big but with paper-thin walls and probably drafty windows, too. She even has a wreath on her door, like we have on ours, except ours is green and red and hers is blue and white with a plastic menorah glued on top. And as soon as we walk into the kitchen, I swear for a second that I'm actually in my own house: countertop covered in flour, eggshells cracked in the sink, butter softening in a patch of sunlight, and a woman in an apron fluttering around, trying to keep everything in order. And that's when we hear a scream coming from the living room.

"AAAAAAAAAAAAAH!" A boy who looks like he can't be older than six or seven runs into the kitchen wearing a Darth Vader mask and carrying a lightsaber.

"Damien!" says the woman in the apron. "I need your help stirring!"

The tiny Darth Vader drops his lightsaber on the floor and runs over to the counter to help.

"That's my little brother," says Vee, shaking her head like she's both embarrassed and proud. "And that's my Tía Rosa."

Tía Rosa looks over her shoulder and waves. "I'd come say hi, but if I let go of this little guy, we're going to have a disaster on our hands."

As Vee and I peel off our outer layers, Vee asks, "Where's Mom?"

"Should be upstairs," says Vee's dad, also pulling off his jacket.

Vee runs into the hall and up the stairs, and I follow her. "Your mom?" I ask. "I thought you said your mom was . . ."

But before I can finish that sentence, a woman walks out of a bedroom wearing bright blue scrubs.

"Hi," I say. "I'm Hannah."

"Hi, Hannah," says the woman. "I'm Vee's mom. You can call me Ezter! I've heard so much about you. I wish I could stay and chat, but I'm already late for work." She bends down and kisses Vee on top of her head, puts on her own jacket, and walks out the door.

"Wait," I say. "If your mom is . . . you know . . . not here anymore . . . then who is that woman?"

"A ghost," Vee says without missing a beat, her face so serious I almost believe her.

She lets out a snort-laugh. "Oh my god, did you actually believe me?" She slaps her thigh with her palm. "She's my stepmom. Technically. She's Damien's mom-mom. But I call her mom because . . . well . . . she's my mom! Even if she's not my, like, birth mom."

"Oh," I say. "That makes sense, I guess."

Vee's grabbing at her necklace beneath her hoodie again, and I reach my hand into my pocket to squeeze mine, too. I haven't shown my necklace to anyone yet, but for some reason, now feels like a good time to show it to Vee. So I pull it out of my pocket. "My grandma gave me this for Hanukkah this year. Did your birth mom give you yours?"

Vee looks at the star in her hand as though she's surprised that she's holding it. "Oh no." She laughs. "My mom gave it to me. Stepmom, I mean. Ezter." She waves her hand in the air, as if clearing away any confusion. "My birth mom wasn't Jewish."

"Wait—really? I thought you said *you* were Jewish."

"I am," Vee says. "I mean, technically, my dad's family is Catholic, and so was my birth mom's, I guess, but I don't think either of them ever did anything Catholic. Besides, my dad married my mom—Ezter, I mean—when I was, like, three, and I've been going to temple ever since." She shrugs, like that's the end of that.

"So—wait." I put my necklace back in my pocket. "Your birth mom wasn't Jewish?"

"Do you need to get your ears checked?" Vee asks. "No, my birth mom wasn't Jewish."

I nod, but slowly, because something isn't quite adding up. "So, did you convert?" I ask. "To Judaism?"

"Convert?" Vee cocks her head at me. "Why would I need to convert? Convert from what?"

"Um . . ." I say. "Catholic?"

"But I was never Catholic."

"I thought you said your parents were."

"Hardly! And even if they were, that doesn't mean *I* am. I don't think I've ever even been to a Catholic church!"

"But that doesn't matter, does it? If your parents are Catholic, you're Catholic."

"Hannah, I brought you here to bake with me today. Not to debate my, like, genealogy."

"I'm just trying to understand!" I say.

Vee sighs. "I'm not sure what about this is hard to understand. And I'm especially not sure why this is any of your business . . ."

"So you've never officially converted, then. Right?"

Vee crosses her arms over her chest. "Hannah . . ."

"But aren't you supposed to?"

Vee raises her eyebrows. "*Supposed* to? Says who? Are you a rabbi now? Are you deciding whether I'm Jewish enough to join your temple?"

"Oh, come on, that's not what I meant." I can tell she is starting to misunderstand me. "Hear me out."

Vee doesn't say anything, so I keep talking.

"If your birth mom wasn't Jewish," I continue, "and if you didn't convert, then you're not really Jewish, right? So don't you need to convert in order to fix that—"

Vee cuts me off. "Wait, wait, wait," she said. "I think I misheard you. Can you repeat that?"

"What?" I try to remember the last thing I said. "I said your birth mom wasn't Jewish?"

"No." Vee squints her eyes at me, and I'm starting to think she's mad at me. "I thought I heard you say *I* wasn't really Jewish. But I couldn't have heard right, because that's an incredibly mean thing for you, of all people, to say to someone."

A peach pit takes root in my throat and I try to swallow it. Did I say Vee wasn't really Jewish? That's the same thing Shira said to me, the same thing that made me so mad at her. "No, no. You're misunderstanding me," I say. "I just meant, like, *biologically* Jewish. Because Judaism comes from the mom, right? So, like I'm Jewish because my mom is Jewish. And Shira's Jewish because her mom is Jewish. And I guess Damien would be Jewish too, because your stepmom is his biological mom."

"She's my *mom*."

"Right, right, but your biological mom wasn't Jewish, so you're not, like, *biologically* Jewish. I didn't mean it as a bad thing. Sorry if it came across that way."

I shrug, like it's no big deal, and for a second, I think I've fixed it. I've talked my way out of potentially hurting my friend's feelings, but all it takes is one look at Vee's face to know that far from getting myself out of a hole, I may have dug myself in deeper.

Vee's face melts into a sarcastic smile, and she laces her fingers beneath her chin like she's praying. "Oh, I'm *so glad* you didn't mean it as a bad thing. *Such* a relief. See, I didn't realize Judaism had to be *biological!* Please forgive me for not running my DNA by you before I started talking about who I am. Because being Jewish certainly doesn't have anything to do with, I dunno, *practicing Judaism,* or *loving God,* or *feeling Jewish.*"

"No, wait," I say, panicking. I have to undo this. I've already lost Shira, I can't lose Vee too. "I didn't mean it as a bad thing. You know, I meant *really* Jewish. Not 'really Jewish.' It's just . . . I dunno . . . the rule!"

"The *rule?*" Vee says. "Whose rule? Yours? Mine? God's? Or is it the rule that *some rabbis*—not all!—use to decide who does and does not get to call themselves Jewish? Do you know where that rule comes from? Do you agree with it? Do you know how many Jews in the world *disagree* with it? Because if you haven't given it any thought, then *you* don't get to rule me out of being Jewish. There are enough people in the world who will do that for you, and they don't need you as their lawyer." Her chin is set now, tight and unmoving, and she looks like she might cry. "Jews get so much hate from the outside. Why do we bring it into the inside too?"

"Wait—" I say, frantic. "Hate? What are you talking about? No one hates you! *I* don't hate you. You're completely mis-understanding what I'm trying to tell you! I'm your friend, Vee! I'm—"

"Ugh!" She groans deep in her throat, and it shuts me up. "A friend wouldn't treat me like this! So just stop talking, Hannah! Stop talking for once!" Vee looks like she might cry now. Tears are brimming and her cheeks are flushed. "Of course people hate us! Of course people hate *me!* And when you say things like that, when you pretend to know who is and who isn't really Jewish because of some 'rule' that you learned without ever thinking about it, then you're just as bad as they are."

"Wait, who's *they?*" I ask. But Vee isn't listening to me anymore.

"You think being Jewish is all about what's in your blood or what's in your head, and that might be a part of it, but it's not all of it. Being Jewish is about what's in your heart, and *you* are not God. You don't know my heart."

Vee wipes her eyes with the backs of her hands, and even though she's standing up straight and tall, something about her posture reminds me of a lava cake after its insides have all oozed out. She sighs, as if she doesn't want to say what she's about to say. "Can you call your grandma to come take you home?"

"Wait, no!" I say, panicking. "I'm sorry! I want to fix this! How can I fix this?"

But Vee is already going down the stairs. "You need to answer that for yourself." She walks back into the kitchen, where everyone is happily making buñuelos, and hands me my jacket. "Hannah has a stomachache," she says to her dad. "Can she call her grandmother?"

"Oh," says Vee's dad, wrinkling his eyebrows in concern. "Sorry to hear that. Yeah, of course."

And when Grandma Mimi shows up a short while later, Vee walks me to her front door. "I'm sorry," I say again.

But Vee shakes her head. "I don't think you're sorry yet. I think you still believe what you said. Let me know when you don't anymore."

She starts to close the door, but as she's turning away, I hear her say one more thing, under her breath.

"I knew it was a bad idea to try to make friends here."

The door is closed now, and I'm left staring at the blue and white Hanukkah wreath on top of the yellow door.

Right

"You have a stomachache?" Grandma Mimi asks, and I nod. It's not a lie, either. At this point I do have a stomachache.

"Grandma Mimi?" I ask. "Isn't it true that Judaism passes through the mother's side?"

Grandma Mimi pats my knee and says, "Of course, bubbelah. Why do you ask?"

I pull my knees up to meet my chin. "No reason."

So Right

Grandma Mimi said I was right.
I knew she would.
She's told me before:
being Jewish comes from the mom.

But if I was right, why do I feel so
wrong?

Wrong

That wrongness itches at me all night. I try to make it go away
by reciting my Torah portion in my head to help me fall asleep,
but no matter how loud I think it, Vee's words echo in my
brain.

You are not God.
But I was right.
Practicing Judaism.
Grandma Mimi said I was right.
Loving God.
Judaism comes from the mother.
Feeling Jewish.
If I could just sit Vee down
You
and explain to her what I meant
   don't
she'll forgive me.
      know
She's going to forgive me.
         my
She has to forgive me.
           heart.

And everything will go back to normal.

You are not God.

I fell asleep, I guess, because it's morning, and my hand hurts from squeezing my necklace so hard, but I don't remember ever grabbing it. As I get ready for school, I think about what I'm going to say to Vee when I see her. But when I finally get to school, she avoids me. In social studies, she sits on the opposite side of the room, partnering with Kyle Goldstein of all people, leaving me to pair up with Patrick Spence, who I literally haven't spoken to since kindergarten. At lunch, I go look for her in our usual classroom, but she isn't there. And every time I see her in the hallway, she pretends she can't hear me say her name and she escapes in the other direction. Once, during pass period, I see her at her locker. Her back is facing me, so I figure I can get close enough to apologize before she can run away, but as soon as I'm within apologizing distance, I run into Shira.

Literally.

"Ow," I say, picking myself up off the floor. "Sorry about that."

Shira dusts off the backs of her jeans. "It's fine. You okay?"

"Sure."

Shira says something else after that, but I don't hear what it is because I'm already standing on my tiptoes looking for Vee. "Do you see Vee anywhere?" I ask.

"Who?"

"Never mind," I say. It's too late anyway. Vee's gone.

"Aunt Yael?" I ask when I see her at my lesson on Thursday. "Judaism comes from the mother, right?"

Aunt Yael puts down the cookie she's eating—oatmeal chocolate chip—and says, "Technically. According to Jewish law, anyway."

"So if someone's mom wasn't Jewish, that means they're also not Jewish. Right?"

Aunt Yael smiles her teacher smile, and I think maybe I'm about to get more than I bargained for with this question.

"Well, what do you think makes someone Jewish?" she asks.

I bite my lip. "Grandma Mimi says if your mom is Jewish, you're Jewish."

"And do you agree with that?"

"I'm not sure."

"Well, how about this." Aunt Yael takes a sip from her glass of milk. "Do you think you're Jewish?"

This feels like a trick question. "Yes?"

"Why?"

I *knew* it was a trick question.

"Because my mom is Jewish?"

"Is your mom Jewish?"

Now, that's definitely a trick question. Because Grandma Mimi would say she is, but Mom would say she isn't. And I'm not sure who gets to decide.

"Sort of?"

I expect Aunt Yael to push me on that, to get me to come up with a real answer, but she doesn't. Instead she says, "Do you think you'd be any less Jewish if your dad was the sort-of-Jewish one instead of your mom?"

"No?" I say. But that's not what Grandma Mimi would say. And probably not what Shira would say, either. But why should it matter which parent is which? I get my frizzy hair from my mom, but my need for braces from my dad. Why should other parts of me be any different? "I'm not asking about when one parent is Jewish," I say. "I'm asking about what happens if neither parent is Jewish. Or when neither *birth* parent is Jewish. Or — I guess what I mean is, can someone be Jewish just because the person they think of as their mother is Jewish, even if their birth mother wasn't?"

Aunt Yael smiles at me. "What does it mean to be a mother? What does it mean to be Jewish?"

I groan. Now we're talking in circles.

"My friend—well, I'm not sure if she's really my friend anymore—she says being Jewish is practicing Judaism, loving God, and feeling Jewish."

"Do you practice Judaism?" Aunt Yael asks. "Do you love God? Do you feel Jewish?"

"I don't know!" I say. "I don't know, I don't know, I don't know! My mom won't let me practice Judaism, I have no idea what people mean when they say God, much less if I *love* God, and how am I supposed to know if I feel Jewish when I don't know what being Jewish feels like!"

She must sense my frustration because she puts her hand on my elbow. "Relax, Hannah," she says. "These aren't easy questions. You aren't supposed to have answers readily available."

I wave her comforting words away. "Don't try to make me feel better. I know what I'm supposed to say."

"Oh, you do, do you?"

"Of course!" I throw my hands in the air. "I know I'm supposed to say I practice Judaism every time I make a batch of sufganiyot, and I love God whenever I get that tingly feeling when I'm singing my Torah portion. And I clearly *must* feel Jewish, since I cared enough about Judaism to spend all my free time preparing for a bat mitzvah no one wanted me to have in the first place."

Aunt Yael is quiet for a moment. Then she says, "This is what you're *supposed* to say?"

I nod.

"Who do you think wants you to say this?"

I shrug. "I don't know. You? Other rabbis? Jews?"

Aunt Yael smiles a small smile. "I assure you, what you're saying is *not* what a lot of rabbis—or a lot of Jews—want you to be saying. And even if you're saying something I agree with now, I wouldn't have agreed with you just a few years back. So there is nothing here that you are *supposed* to be saying."

I roll my eyes, but Aunt Yael shakes her head. "No, Hannah, don't do that. Don't dismiss it like that. *Think* about it. That's all I want from you. These are important questions. They're *hard* questions. They're questions Jewish scholars spend entire lifetimes trying to answer. Orthodox Jews believe one thing, Conservative Jews another, Reform Jews a third, and even *within* these communities there's debate. A *lot* of debate. Two Jews, three opinions, as they say. But what I'm trying to get you to do here, with the short time I have with you, is to give you the tools you need to answer these questions for yourself.

"If you want to practice Judaism, practice it *your* way. If you want to love God, love God the way *you* want to. If you feel Jewish, then be Jewish the way only *you* can."

I stare at my fingers. I don't have anything to say to that.

"You don't look like you believe me," Aunt Yael says eventually.

"I want to believe you. But I guess . . ." My voice trails off. "I guess I *don't* feel Jewish most of the time. My friend said Judaism is about what's in your heart, not about what's in your blood or what's in your head. And I know I'm supposed to believe her—to believe you. I even *want* to believe. It would be so nice if all I need to do is decide I'm Jewish, and poof! There it is! I'm magically Jewish!

"But if I was Jewish, way down deep in my heart, would I be questioning it this much?

"I have no idea what's in my heart. I know what's in my blood, and I can change what's in my head by studying and practicing and learning my Torah portion.

"But my heart? How am I supposed to know what's there?

"There are some days when I don't need to think about it, and my heart feels completely Jewish. But other times my heart feels like nothing at all. Or everything all at once. Or something in between.

"And sometimes, all I feel in my heart is . . . sad! Or angry! Or jealous! And when I feel that way, I know everybody was right all along. Shira and Mom and Dad and everyone else. I know I'm not Jewish at all, and I never will be."

Aunt Yael is quiet for a moment, pursing her lips and nodding her head. And when she finally speaks, she asks, "Is that why this bat mitzvah is so important to you?"

I guess I've never thought of it that way, but something about that feels right. "Nobody ever questions whether Shira is Jewish," I say. "No one ever questions whether Grandma Mimi is Jewish, either. Even Mom—who doesn't want to be Jewish—would never have to prove anything. If she decided tomorrow she wanted to be Jewish again, she would be.

"But not me.

"I have to prove it.

"If I have a bat mitzvah, if I stand on that stage at Beth Shalom in front of everybody I know, no one will ever be able to doubt again that I'm Jewish.

"And maybe if no one else doubts it, I won't doubt it anymore, either."

Aunt Yael opens her mouth, as if she's going to say something, before snapping it shut.

"What?"

"No, nothing. It's . . . Hannah . . . You didn't think you were going to hold your bat mitzvah at Congregation Beth Shalom, did you?"

"Ah . . . No?"

"If it were up to me," she continues, "of course you would. But Beth Shalom is a Conservative synagogue, and even at a Reform synagogue they only allow that for people who are members of the temple. Like me or Grandma Mimi or Shira and her family."

"You mean for people who are really Jewish."

"No!" Aunt Yael practically shouts. "No. Not at all. People who *pay temple dues*. And it doesn't matter if your bat mitzvah is in a temple. This is for you and your friends and your family. And if you think about it . . ."

But I don't hear what I'm supposed to be thinking about, because my vision is fuzzing and my eyes are burning like I got habanero juice in them. I focus on my breathing and relax my jaw so I don't cry right here right now.

"You know you don't need a temple to have a meaningful ceremony," Aunt Yael continues. "You can have a meaningful ceremony in your backyard! Or at a restaurant! Or . . . in the parking lot of a McDonald's! Being Jewish doesn't start when you enter a synagogue, Hannah, and it certainly doesn't stop when you leave. When you're Jewish, you're Jewish *everywhere*. Being Jewish is about the choices you make, the life you lead. You eat Jewishly, you sleep Jewishly, you move through the world Jewishly, and you feel Jewish *every single day*."

But I *don't* feel Jewish! Isn't that the whole point of this bat mitzvah thing? It's supposed to *make* me feel Jewish! "Whatever," I say, swallowing the lump in my throat. "I never even expected to have my bat mitzvah at the temple. I'm not stupid."

Aunt Yael gives me apology eyes and an apology arm pat and hands me what I can only assume is an apology cookie. "I am proud of you, Hannah. You don't need a temple. What matters is the work you've done. And you've done a lot! You've worked so hard and you've come so far, and I just wish I could be there to see you on your big day."

I nearly choke on my apology cookie.

"What do you mean you *wish* you could be there?"

Aunt Yael looks confused. "I . . . your mom. She doesn't . . . I thought—"

No.

No temple *and* no rabbi?

That's not a bat mitzvah at all—that's a birthday party with some Hebrew thrown in. Oh no, oh no, this whole bat mitzvah thing is turning into a recipe for disaster. I'm going to be the laughingstock of the school, and any hopes I ever had of doing this for real have been washed down the drain like dirty dishwater and

no

no

no

a thousand times no

I'm not going to let this bat mitzvah slip away from me. Not after how hard I've worked. Not after losing Shira, and Vee, and any hope of having it in a temple.

My rabbi needs to be there.

My aunt needs to be there.

I will do whatever I need to do to make sure Aunt Yael is there.

"Oh, you're worried about Mom?" I snort. "You don't have to be. Grandma Mimi talked to her!"

Aunt Yael's eyebrows make stiff peaks.

"I swear! Grandma Mimi talked to her last night. I totally forgot because it, like, *just* happened, but it's fine! I mean, not like *fine* fine. It's not like Mom forgives you all the way or anything, but she's fine with you, like, being in the house. As long as it's for an important event. Like a bat mitzvah. And besides, I need you with me or else it's not a real bat mitzvah."

"Hannah, you know that's not true—"

"Just be there. Don't worry about Mom, she's fine. Please . . . make sure you're there."

Aunt Yael breaks off a piece of cookie and puts it in her mouth. "All right, all right. I believe you. I'll be there."

So Wrong

It's not a lie. Not an all-the-way lie or anything, because it's more of a pre-truth. Grandma Mimi did promise she would talk to Mom, and the bat mitzvah is in less than three months, so time is running out.

"Hey, Grandma Mimi?" I ask as she drives me home from Aunt Yael's that night. "Have you talked to Mom yet? You know, about the bat mitzvah stuff?"

Grandma Mimi takes a long time to answer. "Hannah, I promise. I will talk to your mother. Just be patient, okay?"

And I believe her, because Grandma Mimi has never been wrong before. So that night I continue to practice my Torah portion as usual, but after my talk with Aunt Yael, Vee's voice in my ears is even louder than it was last night.

Practicing Judaism, Hannah.

And I'm trying to practice Judaism.

I really am.

But no one is helping me!

My bat mitzvah won't be in a temple.

My parents still don't know about it.

And if Aunt Yael doesn't show up, I won't have a rabbi!

Loving God, Hannah.

What does *God* mean, anyway?

Should I believe in God?

Do I have to believe in God?

Wouldn't a real Jew believe in God?

Wouldn't a real Jew know the answers to these questions?

Feeling Jewish, Hannah.

Vee can't be right.

She can't be.

If she's right, and being Jewish is more than who your mother is and how much Hebrew you can learn, maybe everyone was right all along and I'm not really Jewish after all!

You're not Jewish, Hannah.

You're not Jewish, Hannah.

You're not Jewish, Hannah.

Who am I kidding?

I'm not Jewish at all.

So, So Wrong

I wake up to the sound of my alarm and the smell of breakfast, but my stomach is too knotted up to eat.

I try to relax in the car on the way to school by following the houses as we drive past them.

There's the house with the gardens, which at this point are covered in snow.

There's the house that's always under construction, where the family still hasn't taken down their Christmas decorations.

There's the house with the yellow door—

Wrong, Wrong, Wrong

That's when I see it.
The house with the yellow door.
Vee's house.
The house that is home to my friend,
   the one I said
   wasn't really Jewish,
has a blue and white Hanukkah wreath
   on the porch
torn
down
and has been marked
by a freshly painted
symbol

of hate.

Recipe for Hate

Four lines
bent like spider legs
that meet in the middle.

A symbol
painted in black
full of poison
unmoving
but ready to bite.

The Symbol

Grandma Mimi must not see it, because she drives right by it,
skipping the turn to Shira's house and driving me straight to
school.

I must have imagined it.
I must have.
Because why on earth
would someone have done that?
In our neighborhood.

Today.

I've never seen that symbol outside of a history book
or a black-and-white movie
or *maybe* an article
we had to read during current events.

But that sort of thing is long ago
And, if not that, at least
far away.

So I must have imagined it.

I definitely imagined it.

I one hundred percent, absolutely, for certain

imagined it.

Imagined

But when Vee doesn't show up to school that day
I worry.

"Ms. Shapiro, is Vee—I mean, is Victoria okay? I haven't seen her."
"I'm sure she's fine," Ms. Shapiro says. "But she is marked as absent today."

And that's when I know for sure.

I didn't imagine anything.

Dear Students,

We take both the physical and emotional safety of our student body seriously, and as a result, we have a zero-tolerance policy for hate speech of any kind. This includes, but is not limited to, vandalism, harassment, and destruction of property. For more information regarding our policies, please consult your student handbook . . .

Not Enough

An email?
That's all our school will do?
Send a measly email?

It's not enough.
It's not enough!
It's not
even close
to enough.

I bet no one read that email.
I bet they deleted it before they opened it.
Because no one is talking about it in school
and the teachers don't acknowledge it.

No one is finding out who did this to Vee
or preventing it from happening again.
No one is even *discussing* what happened
or
who it happened to
or
how whoever did it

didn't knock on Vee's door first
and ask

"Are you *biologically* Jewish?"
"Do you *feel* Jewish?"
"Have you had a *bat mitzvah*?"

Sam was right.
We don't always get a choice.

All this person did was
see a blue and white wreath
and hate it.

So they hurt Vee.

And when they hurt Vee

they hurt me too.

Recipe for Falling

Mix together:
Feeling like crying.
Feeling like puking.
Feeling like screaming.
Feeling like I want to see Vee
but also like she doesn't want to see me
and also like I don't want to see me either.

Wanting to apologize.
Wanting to tell her I get it now.
Wanting to say who she is is her choice
but also how the people who attacked her home
didn't give her a choice
and how a few days ago
I didn't give her a choice
and how the thought
that I have anything in common with
whoever hurt her
makes me feel like crying
and puking
and screaming.

Knowing I need to talk about this
with the person who understands me
better than anyone else in the world.

Grandma Mimi.

. . . Falling . . .

"Hey, uh, Hannah?"

"Shira? What's going on?"

"I know things are kind of weird between us, but I got a text from my mom."

"Oh . . . kay . . ."

"She wanted me to tell you she's going to pick you up from school today.

"Me too.

"No bus.

"Okay?"

. . . Falling . . .

The drive home is quiet.
No one will tell me what's going on.
Shira looks worried and nervous, too,
but she isn't talking.

And this time I don't think it's because she's mad.

Vee's front door is no longer yellow.
It's black.

No more symbol.
No more Hanukkah wreath.
No more yellow door.
I squeeze the necklace in my pocket
so hard I draw blood
and close my eyes.

I don't want to look at it.

But with my eyes closed
I hear something.
A thin, wailing sound

a flute song
like a sob.

I hold on to the song
for as long as I can
even after we're too far away
for me to hear it anymore.

And with my eyes
still squeezed shut
I wait
for the
soufflé
to

f

a

l

l

Fallen

When I get home
Mom
and
Dad
and
Sam
are home
early.

"What's going on?"
I ask.
"Where's Grandma Mimi?"

No one will look at me.

Finally Dad says,
"It was sudden,"
and
"She was fine and then she wasn't,"
and
"She went peacefully."

But I barely hear him
because my ears are ringing
and my mouth tastes like salt
and I squeeze my eyes so hard
I see shapes in the darkness.

Grandma Mimi was a light
and that light
has gone
out

And So

I bake.

Challah, to be specific
since I need to punch something.

I hit the dough
and slap it
and smack it
and roll it so hard
my hands shake.
I knead it
    and knead it
            and knead it
I need it
    and need it
            and need it
but at the end of the day
all I have to show for it
is a loaf of challah that's dense and tough.

It doesn't matter anyway.
I'm too sick to eat it.

And So

I practice.

Shesh shanim tizra sadecha   Six years, plant your fields

Shabaton yihyeh la'arets.   a year of rest for the land.

Vesafarta lecha sheva   You shall count seven
shabtot shanim sheva   sabbatical years, that is,
shanim sheva pe'amim   seven times seven years.

But at the end of the day
all I have to show for it
is vision so blurry
I can't read.

And So

I watch TV.
I read a book.
I play *Zelda, Mario, Tetris,* anything.

But in the end
it doesn't matter what I do
what I play
what I bake
what I sing
because nothing has changed.

Grandma Mimi is gone
and there is nothing I can do about it.

Funeral

We stand at the front of Congregation Beth Shalom, a line of people waiting to hug us. I stand with Mom, Dad, and Sam on one side of the hall. Aunt Yael stands on the other.

The guests come, one by one.

"She was a light," they say.

"A mensch."

"A true blessing in our lives."

The temple fills up.

Fifty.

Eighty.

A hundred people.

More.

Our New York cousins fly in, and so do the ones from San Francisco. They hug us, and it turns out I do remember Drake from when we were little kids.

We make pleasant conversation, forcing smiles onto our faces. I keep my hands around the necklace in my left pocket, and through it all, Mom and Aunt Yael pretend they don't see each other.

I want to scream.

NOW?

You can't put this aside

NOW?

Even Shira and I seem to have reached a truce.

She comes into the receiving line with her parents, and we hug because it seems like that's what we're supposed to do, but it feels stiff and awkward.

I wish Mom and Aunt Yael would do the stiff and awkward thing.

Eventually the receiving line shortens, slows, and stops.

Standing room only in the temple, and the service starts.

We say prayers, tell stories, sing songs, and I can't help but think about how last time we were here, Mom closed her mouth, as if she hated that she knew every word, but now she stares empty.

On that day Dad was checking his phone beneath his leg and Sam was flipping through the pages of his prayer book, but now they both stare too.

Grandma Mimi was to my left, hands open wide, singing as loud as she could, but that spot is emptier than anything now.

Then there's me, Hannah, in the middle of it all, prayer book cracked open on my legs, and for the first time in my entire life I know the words we're speaking. The letters on the page in front of me are like old friends: there's a *yod* here, a *tav* there, a *gimel* and a *kaf* and a *lamed*. Soon the letters aren't letters at all, but words — *Yitgadal v'yitkadash sh'mei raba* — and before I know it, the words on the page become words in my head, become words in my mouth, become words in the air, and I can't seem to shake the idea that the words we're saying now are the same ones we said when Grandpa Joseph died, that Grandma Mimi said when her parents died, that they said when *their* parents died, and that maybe one day my grandkids will say when I die.

And as the voices in the temple rise and fall, it's as if my voice is more than just one voice. It's all the hundreds of voices in the temple, and all the thousands of voices of thousands of people who have *ever* said these words in this temple. It's all the millions of voices that have ever said these words in any temple ever, and all the billions and trillions of voices that will say these words someday in the future. And as the words continue, I raise my voice louder and louder and louder, until I can't contain it anymore.

I feel like a pot of water boiling over.

I sit in the pew, tears falling down my cheeks, in the middle of a room full of people who love my grandmother as much as I do, rocking back and forth, back and forth, back and forth, with the words in my head

echoing
echoing
echoing.

Shiva

Sheva means seven.

I know that from my Torah portion.

  Vesafarta lecha sheva shabtot shanim sheva shanim
                     sheva pe'amim vehayu lecha.

Seven sabbatical years, seven times seven years, that's

sheva

sheva

sheva.

Sheva days to create the earth.

Sheva days in Passover.

Sheva words in the first verse of the Torah, that's

sheva

sheva

sheva.

Sheva means luck.

It means completion.

It means holiness.

Sheva

sheva

shiva.

Shiva means someone has died.

Sitting Shiva

When Grandpa Joseph died, we sat shiva for him, and now we do the same for Grandma Mimi.

Seven days.

Seven days of mourning. Seven days of hanging out in our house while everybody who ever knew Grandma Mimi comes over to pay their respects. Seven days of people bringing us food and trading their stories for our own. Seven days of family time, dedicated to remembering the one we lost.

Seven days, and we can't get through one.

It's early in the morning. People are arriving, slowly at first, then faster and faster, until we can't keep track of who's here anymore. They come dressed in black and telling stories about Grandma Mimi while we eat the casseroles they made for us.

That's when I hear Mom's voice shouting from the foyer, and I wonder if maybe someone spilled something, so I go look for her. But when I find her, she's not alone.

Standing in the frame of our open door
with her hood covered in February snow
is Aunt Yael.

Vinegar

"What are you doing here?" Mom asks.

"Am I early?" Aunt Yael responds. "I thought the shiva started at eight."

"Yes, but why are you *here*?"

"For shiva?" Aunt Yael's voice is tense. "I can come back if I'm early."

"This is *my* house," Mom says. "Mine. And you're not any more welcome here now that Mom is dead than you were when she was alive."

"Wait, I thought—"

"Stop, Yael. I don't want to hear what you *thought*. I have had enough of your excuses and your apologies. I don't want to hear how you've grown, or how you've changed, or how you've *evolved*. I don't want to hear any of it! I want you to leave."

"I'm sorry, I . . ." Aunt Yael's hands shake. "I thought it was okay. I thought she'd talked to you."

"Who?" Mom asks. "Who talked to me?"

Aunt Yael is spluttering now. "I . . . I . . . I . . ." She's confused, as if she hasn't expected this. As if she thought my mother, the woman who hasn't talked to her in practically a decade, would finally be willing to share her house with her at their mother's shiva.

Because I told her Grandma Mimi had talked to Mom.

I told her Mom said it was okay.

Aunt Yael is here today because I lied to her.

Aunt Yael keeps talking. "Oh no . . . I knew it couldn't be true. I knew it. I guess I hoped—"

"Knew *what* wasn't true, Yael?"

They're talking about me, about what I said to Aunt Yael at our last Hebrew lesson, and sure, when I told Aunt Yael that Grandma Mimi had talked to Mom, that Mom would be okay with Aunt Yael showing up at our house, it wasn't meant to be a lie. It was meant to be a pre-truth. Grandma Mimi *was* going to talk to Mom. Mom *was* going to be okay with it. Mom *would* welcome her in our home.

But Grandma Mimi is gone. She never had a chance to talk to Mom.

Should that matter, though? Shouldn't Mom and Aunt Yael realize now is the time to be on the same side? Don't they see we won't make it through this—that *I* won't make it through this—if they can't get along?

This fight has gone on long enough.

I can't tolerate the cracks in the earth anymore.

Grandma Mimi wouldn't *want* me to tolerate the cracks in the earth anymore.

The front door is wide-open, still, and even though the February cold is piercing my sweater, I'm not cold. In fact, I'm hot.

Hot. Like the oven is preheating in the kitchen and a pot of oil is simmering on the stove and Grandma Mimi is standing behind me with a bowl of dough, saying, *You can do this, bubbelah. You've got this. Tell them your truth.*

So I steady my voice, and as loud and strong as I can, I say, "Mom, Aunt Yael is here because of me. I told her to come."

Baking Soda

"Hannah?" Mom looks at me, confused, shocked, hurt. "You talked to her?"

There's a part of me that wants to say no, that wants to dissolve into the wall like a sugar cube in water, but there's another part of me, a bigger part, that knows this is what Grandma Mimi wanted. This is what she was hoping for. I could be the reason they get back together. I could help heal the earth.

"Yes," I say. "Yes, I did. A lot, actually. On Thursday evenings for the past four months. See, Aunt Yael was the only person on the whole entire planet, other than Grandma Mimi, who seemed to think I was Jewish. So every Thursday after school, when you thought I was working on a project, I was actually with her.

"My Aunt Yael.

"Studying for my bat mitzvah."

Boom.

Mom's chin is made of iron.

Of steel.

Of titanium.

"You want to know what happened," Mom says—

—no—

—whispers.

I've never seen her whisper like this before.

I don't like it.

"Mom?" Sam appears at the door. Other guests are peeking their heads in to see what the yelling is all about. "Maybe this isn't a good time—"

Mom puts a hand out. "No. No! I've spent years protecting Hannah from this. Protecting myself from this. But Hannah doesn't want to be protected. No, Hannah wants a bat mitzvah! She wants to hang out with her Aunt Yael! She wants to be *Jewish!*

"Well, if Hannah thinks she can handle the truth, maybe it's time we told her."

Mom says this like she's talking to Sam, but her eyes don't leave me the whole time. "My sister," she continues, "didn't want me to marry your father. Because he wasn't Jewish. Did you know that, Hannah?"

No.

No, I did not know that.

"She didn't come to the wedding. She refused to visit me in the hospital when I had Sam and when I had you. We wouldn't have seen her at all if it weren't for our parents, who tried to keep the family together however possible. But when our father died—at his funeral—she decided that was it. She'd had enough."

Mom's chin isn't iron anymore. Maybe it never was.

Mom's chin is shattered sugar.

She looks at Aunt Yael, whose face is pointed at the ground as if she can't bear to look up, and I hope it stays there. I hope she doesn't look at me.

If she did, I'm not sure I could handle it.

"My own sister," Mom continues, "your precious Aunt Yael, said she no longer recognized me as her family. I'll never forget how she said it, either." Mom looks up for a half second, her eyes dry. "She said I was a 'traitor' to our people, and she didn't want to have anything more to do with me."

Tears are falling from Aunt Yael's chin now.

"You think of Judaism as this amazing thing," Mom continues, "because you love your grandmother—and we all do. But Judaism can be as cruel as anything, and your Aunt Yael is proof of that. I didn't want you to be Jewish, Hannah, because *this* is what it means to be Jewish." She points at Aunt Yael. "The cruelty. The division. The rules and restrictions.

"Judaism makes family turn against family.

"You think I'm so horrible, Hannah, because you think I'm the one who decided I wasn't Jewish. But it wasn't me. It was never me. It was my sister."

As if I didn't already get it, Mom keeps going.

"When she removed herself from the family, when she decided I wasn't Jewish anymore, she didn't mean only me. She meant my family, too. The family that came after me. Do you understand what I'm saying, Hannah?"

She pauses and

I hope

    I hope

        I hope

            she's done speaking—

—but she's not.

The Truth

"It means she doesn't think you're Jewish, either."

Not

It can't be true.

It can't be.

That's not the Aunt Yael I know.

That's not the woman who taught me Hebrew and baked me biscuits with watermelon jelly, who Grandma Mimi drove me to visit every Thursday, who talked about *tikkun olam*, who sent me eight different audio clips of *Behar* and slapped her leg in rhythm when she prayed.

That's not my Aunt Yael.

"Hannah," Aunt Yael says. "Hannah? Hannah, I need you to know I don't believe that anymore. I hate the person I was too. I hate her as much as your mom does."

And I see her apologizing. I see her crying. I see her trying to make things right, but they're all empty words.

Empty, except they confirm what Mom said.

It's true.

Well, someone I once trusted taught me no one on earth owes anybody else forgiveness, so I look Aunt Yael straight in the eyes and say, "I hate you, too."

Because the one person left on earth who I believed actually thought I was Jewish

doesn't.

Alone

I run away.

I jump over piles of shoes in the foyer, push past the black-clad mourners, and launch myself up the stairs. I don't want anybody to see me right now. I want to be alone.

But when I get to my bedroom, someone's there. I know it's impossible, but for a split second I think it's Grandma Mimi, waiting on my bed to hold me and stroke my hair and say, *Oy! Stop crying, eh? Let's make some sufganiyot and talk this out.*

But she's not there.

Of course she's not there.

She'll never be there again.

The person in my room is not Grandma Mimi, the person I most want to see right now. Instead, it's the last person I want to see.

Shira.

"Hannah?" she says.

I stop dead in my tracks. I didn't realize she was here in my house, much less here in my bedroom. "Get out," I say.

She gets off the bed and approaches me carefully. "Hannah, I'm sorry about . . . what happened."

I shake my head. I don't know what she's referring to—to Grandma Mimi, to us, to something else entirely—and quite honestly, it doesn't matter. My face is red and salty with tears, and the very last thing I need right now is another fight.

"Get out," I say again.

Shira walks toward me, slowly, slowly. "Hannah, I heard what happened downstairs, and I—"

"I know!" I shout. "You were right, okay? It was never real! It was all a big lie! My 'bat mitzvah' was never going to be in a temple, my own rabbi wouldn't have been able to come, and even my parents didn't know about it! I lied to you, and to my family, and to our friends, and to everyone! I was being selfish! This whole time I was being greedy and selfish and jealous. Because you were right. I never went with you to temple, I never asked about Hebrew school, and even now, after all this time, I still have no idea if I believe in God. So you win, Shira. Okay? Are you happy now? I'm not really Jewish, and I never was."

"Hannah—"

"Stop." I put my hand up. "Please, if you ever were my best friend, you won't say I told you so. You won't rub it in my face. You'll leave my room right now and never talk to me again."

Shira stands stone-still for a moment and nods once. "Okay," she says, and leaves.

Now I really am alone.

Traitor

I guess we had more guests at our house, but I don't remember when they arrived and I don't remember when they left. I just know that now it's the middle of the night and I'm upstairs in our drafty attic, with Aunt Yael's words pounding in my head.

Traitor

Traitor   *Traitor*

I'm standing in the attic

Traitor   over a box filled with dreck.   *Traitor*

I reach my hand into my pocket

Traitor   pull out the necklace   *Traitor*

Traitor   open my hand   *Traitor*

and the necklace

Traitor   f   *Traitor*

a

l

l

s

Recipe for Winter

Mix together:
one (1) dad
    who wakes up at 5 a.m. to beat traffic
    who comes home at 8 p.m.
    with a sackful of McDonald's cheeseburgers
        or Chinese takeout
        or greasy pizza
        that will be our dinner.
one (1) mom
    whose face is gray
    whose eyes are red
    who disappears into her home office
        when she's not at the university.
one (1) Sam
    who leaves the house before I'm awake
    who comes back after I'm asleep
    who I swear I haven't seen once
        since the shiva ended.
one (1) Hannah
    who can't look Vee in the eyes
        without feeling sick
    who can't look Shira in the eyes

without feeling sick

who takes the bus to school now

and passes by Vee's front door

painted

black

every single day

and feels

sicker than sick.

one (1) Hannah

who doesn't deserve to bake

one (1) Hannah

who doesn't deserve to practice her Hebrew

one (1) Hannah

who has barely seen another human

all

winter

long.

one (1) email

from Aunt Yael

that gets read exactly one

(1)

time

and

trashed.

Dear Hannah,

I know you don't want to hear from me, and I don't blame you for that. I don't want to make excuses for what I said years ago. There are none — I meant what I said when I said it.

I used to be a person who thought I was better than other people because of how I practiced my religion. That I was superior, closer to God, than people who practiced differently. Your mom is someone who practiced differently, and at the time, I saw that as weakness. As a betrayal. As illegitimacy.

I need you to know that as time has passed, I no longer believe those things. I know my words now can't undo the words I once said, and I know you do not need my permission to be who you truly are, but I do see you as Jewish. You, and your brother, and your mother, and even, in many ways, your father.

I guess I hoped that if I practiced with you for your bat mitzvah, I might be able to undo some of the hurt I caused your family. I know Grandma Mimi believed that as well, but I see now we were wrong. We were only making things worse. And for that, I'm eternally sorry.

I understand if you never want to see me again, and this will be the last you hear from me, unless you reach out.

I love you, Hannah. You've done incredible work these past few months. You've learned more than I could have ever hoped, and no matter what you choose to do, I will be celebrating your bat mitzvah in the spring.

Love,

Aunt Yael

Spring

Spring

Spring is when we make macaroons.

Made.

Spring used to be when we made macaroons.

Coconut cookies dipped in chocolate, which means this time of year the house should smell like milk, and chocolate, with a hint of coconut.

But today the house doesn't smell like anything. In fact, the house hasn't smelled like anything except takeout containers since shiva ended. Since my family started spending as little time together as humanly possible. Since I stopped whisper-singing my Torah portion. Since Sam's college decisions appeared in the mail—big envelopes, all of them—and reappeared hours later in the recycling bin. Since I saw Vee going into the orchestra room during lunch with Maggie Sakurai and Kwame James, all three of them carrying small black suitcases. Since the first time Shira and I shared a bus ride to school but pretended we didn't see each other.

Since my life fell apart.

I think this is the longest I've ever gone without baking something. Without eating food that didn't come in a container.

Without the house smelling like sugar and vanilla extract and fresh berries from the farmers' market.

Without opening the Big Book of What's Cooking.

It's covered in a layer of dust now. I know the whole point of shiva was for people to bring us food so we didn't have to work while we mourned, but not cooking feels like a death all its own.

The house is supposed to smell like macaroons this time of year, like springtime. It's supposed to smell like new beginnings, and warmth and laughter and sunshine, but it doesn't.

Of course it doesn't.

Our house smells like empty.

Secret Projects

They try to make my birthday special.

Sam bakes me a cake, but I can manage only a few bites before my stomach gets too sad to eat.

Mom and Dad give me an iPhone, but phones aren't fun if you have no one to talk to.

Mom asks me if I want to throw a party this weekend, and I almost laugh.

I was supposed to throw a party this weekend. A big party at the temple, where all my friends and family would come together—Mom and Aunt Yael, Sam and Dad, Shira and Vee, and of course, Grandma Mimi—and we would put all our fighting behind us. I was going to sing in a language no one thought I could learn and prove to everybody, once and for all, I was *really* Jewish.

But after what happened with Aunt Yael

and what happened with Shira

and what happened with Vee

and what appeared on her door one day later

and of course, the fact that the one person who was looking forward to my bat mitzvah more than anything else in the world is gone now . . .

. . . well, the idea of a party feels ridiculous.

"May I be excused?" I pick a bit of cake out of my newly tightened braces and go upstairs to sulk in my room.

I'm up there so long I fall asleep, and wake up only when my new phone vibrates.

At first my heart jumps. Maybe this text is from Vee, wishing me a happy birthday and telling me she forgives me for being such a jerk.

Or maybe it's from Shira, wishing me a happy birthday, saying she wants to be friends again, she misses driving to school with me, and she doesn't want to have a break from our friendship anymore.

Or maybe it's from a genie, telling me the past few months of my life never happened, and if I close my eyes and wish hard enough, it will be September again, and we can redo this whole year. And oh, by the way, happy birthday!

I unlock my phone and realize: of course. It's from one of the three people on the entire planet who actually know my phone number:

Sam.

> Whatcha doing?

I knock on the wall that separates our rooms. "You can come in, you know."

Sam finds me not ten seconds later, and this time he says out loud, "Whatcha doing?"

"Homework." It's clearly a lie. I'm not so much as holding a pencil, and I've barely done any homework since Grandma Mimi died.

"Not learning your Torah portion anymore?" Sam asks.

"Very funny."

"I wasn't trying to be funny. I liked hearing you whisper in Hebrew from the next room. Plus, it inspired a few projects of my own."

"What projects?" I ask, eager to change the subject. "Is this why you've been out of the house so much lately?"

"Gotta pay for college," he says. "No— But seriously, you'll find out soon enough."

"Oh, come on," I say. 'Tell me now. It's my birthday!"

Sam checks the time on his phone. "Technically, it isn't anymore."

I groan, and Sam laughs.

"Do you really want to know?" he asks.

I nod.

"How about this. Tomorrow morning, come to Millennium Park. Noon-ish. There's a big event going on there I think you might like. Sound good?"

I raise my eyebrows. "Why can't you tell me now?"

Sam raises his eyebrows right back at me. "Because it'll be more fun to show you."

He leaves my room without giving me another hint, but as I'm drifting off to sleep, my phone vibrates one final time.

You are cordially invited to the

PIE ARE SQUARED SPRING S-PIE-CTACULAR!

Millennium Park
9 a.m.–3 p.m.
Saturday, April 16

BE THERE OR BE SQUARED

Sam's Secret

Millennium Park is crowded on a normal day, but today it's more crowded than I've ever seen it. This pie thingy has taken over the place. Everywhere I look I see people eating squares of pie off compostable plates under banners that say PIE ARE SQUARED SPRING S-PIE-CTACULAR.

I pull out my phone and text Sam.

> I'm at that pie thing. Where are you? Are you working the event somewhere?

That's when I hear a voice.

"Hannah!"

It's Amit, Sam's friend. The one he spent New Year's Eve with. I wave, and he comes running toward me. "Sam's been looking for you!" He adjusts the chef's hat he's wearing. "Come on!"

Amit's moving a million miles a minute, and I practically have to run to keep up. "This is your first one, right?" Amit asks, and I want to respond *One what?* But Amit keeps chattering as he guides me past The Bean, the fountain, and those giant faces that spit water. "I don't know how he kept it a secret from you for so long," Amit babbles. "You're gonna freak!"

I'm a millimeter away from "freaking" for reasons unrelated to Sam, when I finally see Sam himself. He's wearing a chef's hat just like Amit's, along with a matching T-shirt and apron, all stamped with the Pie Are Squared logo—two cartoon guys clinking squares of pie together, saying, "Hear, hear!"

"Hannah!" Sam runs to meet me. He wraps me up in a hug, and I wonder if he's eaten about a thousand of those little pie squares. I can't remember the last time my brother hugged me at all, much less in public.

"Welcome to the Pie Are Squared Spring S-Pie-ctacular!" Sam high-fives Amit, who's laughing hysterically.

"You should see the look on your face!" Amit says to me, and I want to be like *Who are you again?* because somehow this whole thing feels like one elaborate joke.

"What's going on?" I ask Sam. "Have you been working for this Pie Are Squared company to pay for culinary school? Is that why you're never at the house anymore?"

But the more I look around, the more that doesn't feel quite right. First of all, Sam's and Amit's hats are blue, but all the other workers' hats are white.

Also, the two cartoon guys on the Pie Are Squared logo look a little like Sam and Amit.

But the thing that really throws me for a loop is that I recognize a lot of the foods people are eating.

There's pie, but there's more than just pie.

There's challah and baklava and buttermilk biscuits.

And I'd recognize that rugelach anywhere.

I grab a cookie off the table and take a bite. "Will someone explain what is going on?"

But before Sam has a chance to say another word, I see them.

There, walking up the pathway, are the only two people who could make the taste of rugelach in my mouth turn from sweet to bitter.

It's our parents.

Peanut Butter and Caviar

Oh no.

This can't be good.

Grandma Mimi was the only one who could keep the peace between Dad and Sam, and at the end, even she was having trouble. If they start fighting right here, right now, who's going to stop them before it goes sour? This might be the fight that does them in. The one they never recover from.

"Sam?" Dad asks.

Oh boy, Dad does *not* look happy. Even Mom doesn't look happy, and I've always suspected she's secretly been on Sam's side with this whole culinary school business.

"Hannah?" Mom says. "What are you doing here?"

Sam looks at them happily, as if he'd invited them to a surprise birthday party. "You made it!" he says. "You're all here!"

Amit slaps Sam on the back and says, "I'm gonna peace. You good?"

Sam nods, and Amit clears out.

"Sam, do you want to tell us what's going on here?" Mom asks.

Sam clears his throat, as if he's about to recite a prepared speech. "Mom, Dad, Hannah, I wanted to tell you all that as of this morning, I paid the deposit to go to National Hobart

School of Culinary Arts. I officially accepted their offer. I'm going to be a pastry chef."

I expect Dad to get angry. To turn beet red and scream at Sam. But mostly he looks confused.

"Before you say anything," Sam says, "I want to tell you that I paid for it all myself, with my own money. Money I earned from this." He holds his arms out wide, as if he's trying to embrace all of Millennium Park at once. "Pie Are Squared," he continues. "My bakery."

And just like that, something clicks in my head. The banners, the T-shirts, Sam wearing a chef's hat emblazoned with a professionally designed logo showing his and his friend's face.

And of course, that Pie Are Squared seems to be selling Grandma Mimi's rugelach.

Sam doesn't work for Pie Are Squared.

Sam *is* Pie Are Squared.

"Your *what*?" Dad and Mom say in one voice.

"I know how it sounds," Sam says. "But hear me out. It started as a winter break thing. I was going to bake a whole bunch of pies and sell them to the kids at school for the holidays. They were going to be square so I could call myself Pie Are Squared because, you know, it's a math and science school.

"Anyway, it was supposed to be small. I'd make a few hundred bucks, prove that people wanted what I was making. But it didn't take long for it to blow up. Soon I was getting more orders than I could handle, and that's when I roped in Amit. His parents own a restaurant, so we were using their kitchen for a while, but it became clear that we needed something bigger. So we rented this commercial kitchen space, which meant we had to hire more people, and blah blah blah. Ultimately, people loved the food, and the orders kept coming in, so we kept doing it. And now . . ." He spreads his arms out again. "The way things are going, I'll have no trouble paying my way through college."

Dad lets out a single barking laugh. "You seriously think you can pay for college with a pie company? Do you have any idea how much college costs?"

"Do you have any idea how much I've made?"

Dad crosses his arms over his chest. "Okay, I'll play along. How much have you made?" He's grinning like he thinks he's won. Like there isn't an amount of money high enough that could possibly convince him Sam's pie company is worth his time. That any sort of life outside of financial . . .

. . . something-or-other . . .

could be valuable.

But Sam matches Dad's smile, smug for smug, as he reaches into his pocket and pulls out his phone. He thumbs it open, and without touching the screen—as if he planned this, as if he knew it would come down to a number on the screen— he hands the phone to Dad.

Dad's mouth drops open.

"Wh—" Dad blinks, as if whatever he's seeing is a figment of his imagination. "How?"

"How?" Sam says. "Because I'm good at this. Because this is what I'm supposed to be doing. Because maybe your opinion on what is valuable is incomplete. Because maybe you should trust me."

The laughter in Dad's voice is gone as he hands the phone back to Sam. The "I was joking!" wink in his eye has disappeared.

This is uncharted territory for us.

Sam has never gone behind Mom and Dad's back, much less proved Dad wrong.

What if this is the moment Dad snaps?

What if Dad can't stand to be proved wrong and it doesn't matter how much money Sam earned, because it was never about the money at all?

What if Dad will simply never approve of his son becoming a pastry chef?

I wish Grandma Mimi were here.

She'd know how to fix this.

Without her, I don't know if our family can survive another explosion.

But even though Dad is turning tomato red, Sam doesn't fight him. Instead, he simply offers dad a plate. "Pie?" he asks.

I don't expect Dad to take it, not when he's this angry, but he does take it. He takes the plate in his left hand and a fork in his right, and he cuts off a piece, puts it in his mouth, chews, and swallows.

Then?

He smiles.

It's small at first, but it grows bigger and bigger, until he's laughing.

And it's not the mean sort of laughing he does when he's "joking" about something.

It's the "how could I have been so wrong?" kind of laughter. The "how did I not realize this was happening?" kind of laughter. The "my son is actually incredible" kind of laughter.

Dad's laughing so hard that when Mom asks, "What's so funny?" he can barely get a word out. He holds up one finger as if to say *hold on,* and syllable by syllable, he says, "It's . . . really . . . good!"

He dissolves into laughter again, and even though I have absolutely no idea how Sam's pie being good is funny, I laugh too.

And Mom is laughing.

And Sam is laughing.

And this right here?

The four of us laughing over Grandma Mimi's pie?

Maybe she isn't too far away after all.

Recipe for Back to Normal

Mix together

. . .

. . .

. . .

you know what?

I have absolutely no idea.

But whatever happened
it tastes pretty great.

Really Jewish

At the end of the day, Sam and Amit have sold everything. They've amassed enough orders to keep busy through the end of summer, and they made enough money to pay for Sam's entire first year of culinary school.

"Wow," Sam says, scrolling through the order list on his iPad. "I may be so busy with Pie Are Squared, I might not have time for Hobart!"

Dad groans. "Don't even joke about that."

And with one final slice of pie for each of them, Mom and Dad head home while I stay behind with Sam. It's late by the time we're done, and my stomach is growling, so I dig into the small box of rugelach I bought from one of the tents.

"It feels good that people still get to eat her food," I say.

Sam unties his apron. "I think that's why she suggested I do it."

"Wait—" I stop in my tracks. "This was Grandma Mimi's idea?"

Sam smiles and shrugs, like maybe it was, maybe it wasn't. But Sam can be as cryptic as he wants, because I know the truth.

This was her plan all along.

She knew Sam had it in him. All he needed was someone to give him permission.

"I'm glad I know that," I say. "I think Grandma Mimi would be happy to know at least one of her secret plots was successful this past year."

"What do you mean at least one?"

"Well"—I cough into my arm—"at least you get to be a pastry chef, since my bat mitzvah was an epic failure."

Now it's Sam's turn to stop in his tracks. "Why do you say it was an epic failure?"

I laugh once, like a bark. "Epic failure" was meant to be an understatement. My thirteenth birthday had come and gone, Mom pitched a fit when she found out I was studying behind her back with Aunt Yael, and between losing Shira, Vee, and Grandma Mimi—the people I would most want to share the day with—yeah, I would say it was an epic failure.

But I don't know how to say all that to Sam, so instead I say, "Oh, come on. You know as well as I do the idea was stupid. No one would have let me have a bat mitzvah anyway. And let's face it. I was never *really* Jewish."

Sam looks at me like I told him chocolate is a vegetable. "Who says you're not really Jewish?"

My throat is tightening all of a sudden, and after having such a good day, it feels silly to be crying right now. So I swallow hard. "Everybody says it. Mom and Dad don't want me to be Jewish, Shira has made it crystal clear how she feels, and you saw what happened with Aunt Yael."

Sam squints at me in the dim light. "Look, I know it hurts when your own friends and family don't accept who you are. Believe me, I get it. But if Mom and Dad and Shira don't think you're Jewish, who cares? That says more about them than it does about you."

"But Aunt Yael doesn't think I'm Jewish. She said—"

"Oh, who cares what Aunt Yael said *seven years ago?*"

I reach for the necklace in my pocket, and then I remember it's not there anymore.

"Sure," Sam continues. "Seven years ago Aunt Yael thought you weren't Jewish. Seven *years*. But now? You really think the woman who sobbed in our living room while you learned about what might be the worst thing she's done in her life doesn't think you're Jewish? And even if she doesn't. Even if she still believes what she once thought . . . don't *you* think you're Jewish?"

"Well"—I shrug—"I never actually had my bat mitzvah, so . . ." But even as the words come out of my mouth, they don't feel right. After all that's happened—singing Hebrew at Grandma Mimi's funeral, finding out about Mom and Aunt Yael, seeing the horrible symbol that appeared on Vee's door—it feels like maybe bat mitzvahs don't have nearly as much to do with being Jewish as I originally thought.

I almost want Sam to ignore what I just said, but he doesn't. "Oh, *come on!*" He shakes his head. "Now you're being intentionally obtuse. There are so many Jewish people in the history of the world who never had a party to celebrate their coming of age, and that doesn't make them any less Jewish. Think of all the Jews who turned thirteen while they were fleeing Egypt, or while they were imprisoned in concentration camps, or while they were growing up in oppressive school systems where something as simple as wearing a kippah could get them bullied, harassed, or worse! Your own grandmother never even had a bat mitzvah because the patriarchy decided that women weren't *holy enough* to read the Torah! So if you seriously think that not having a bat mitzvah means you're not Jewish, you learned less from your sessions with Aunt Yael than I thought you did."

And he's right.

Sam is one hundred percent, totally right.

And as I make my way home beside my brother, who teamed up with my grandmother to pay his way through culinary school, I realize something.

Maybe it was never about the party at all.

An Idea

That night, we cook dinner for the first time since Grandma Mimi died.

Spaghetti and meatballs, with a dessert of our springtime treat: coconut macaroons.

Nothing we're making is terribly fancy, and it's certainly not up to our usual standards, but even though I'm tired from the long day, it feels good to be back in our kitchen. To dust off the Big Book of What's Cooking and give our oven a workout. Sort of like stretching after a long night's sleep.

I'm on macaroon duty, mixing coconut and condensed milk in the bowl while Sam is shaping meatballs. Mom is boiling tomatoes for sauce, and we even managed to get Dad involved, though he's mostly heating water while checking his phone.

"I'm leaving the cooking to the pros!" Dad says, and he winks at Sam, who smiles big since I guess he is actually a pro now.

"Richard, your water is boiling over!" Mom turns down the heat on the stove before it makes a mess everywhere.

"Don't blame me. Blame your mother, who never taught me advanced cooking techniques, like boiling water."

Sam laughs. "She probably knew you couldn't handle it."

I check on the macaroons in the oven, and it looks like they're about done—crisp, golden brown on top, cooked all the way through. I take them out of the oven and let them cool on the countertop, and for about the millionth time tonight I wish Grandma Mimi were here to see this. The four of us making a meal together, quiet, tired, and happy.

"You know, Hannah," says Mom, reaching back to tie her hair into a braid. "Grandma Mimi made macaroons for my bat mitzvah."

I stop mixing. "She did?"

Mom raises her eyebrows. "Does that surprise you?"

"I'm not surprised she made you macaroons. I'm surprised you're talking about your bat mitzvah."

Mom laughs. "My mom made a lot of food for my bat mitzvah. I mean a *lot*. Macaroons and rugelach and sufganiyot. Hamantaschen, apple-honey challah, babka . . . basically, my bat mitzvah was one giant dessert bar. Of course I wanted it to be catered by a fancy cupcake company, but Mom insisted. She said the day was supposed to be about family and tradition, and one day I'd thank her for it." Mom finishes tying off her hair and pops a hunk of coconut into her mouth. "I never did thank her for it," she finishes sadly.

And all at once an idea hits me.

"Mom!" In my excitement I have to stop myself from knocking over the macaroon tray. My mind is racing now—rugelach! sufganiyot! hamantaschen! challah!—and it takes everything in me not to jump up onto my chair and dance the hora right there in the kitchen.

I take a deep breath to calm myself, and then I say, "What if it's not too late?"

Macaroons

4C fresh coconut ← grated and toasted
1/3 C sugar
1/4C condensed milk
pinch salt
1t vanilla
2 egg whites
chocolate

Mix coconut, ~~condesned~~ condensed milk, sugar, salt, and
vanilla in one bowl, and in another, beat egg whites
to stiff peaks. Add coconut mixture to egg whites and
scoop onto a cookie tray. Bake at 375 until golden brown
and dip in melted chocolate.

Remember:

Use fresh coconut
for a fresh start.

Operation Bat Mitzvah

Sam was right. It doesn't matter what other people think about whether or not I'm Jewish, because I *do* think I'm Jewish.

I don't need a party to tell me that.

The further I get from it, the more it feels as if the image I had in my head—going to a temple, standing in front of all my friends, and dancing the night away—doesn't fit me.

That was Shira's night.

Not mine.

But that doesn't mean I can't put everything I've learned over the past few months to good use.

Maybe it's better to make the tradition match our lives instead of making our lives match the tradition.

And this time I tell Mom my idea. Because I've learned my lesson. I'm not going forward with this unless everyone is onboard. And maybe it's because it's finally right, but tonight, Mom gives permission easily.

With a pinch in her voice she says, "You know, I think she would have loved that."

And it's settled.

Operation Bat Mitzvah is back on track!

Hannah Malfa-Adler invites you

to celebrate her grandmother

Miriam Adler

being called to the Torah

as a bat mitzvah

JUNE 10, AT 7:30 P.M.
for Shabbat dinner
(and small ceremony)
at Hannah's house

2378 41st St., Chicago, IL
RSVP 773 207 1128

Korach

There's a lot to prepare before Grandma Mimi's bat mitzvah. There's a menu to plan, and Shabbat equipment to find in the attic, and of course, I need to practice for the ceremony.

So that night, even though I'm exhausted from Millennium Park and cooking dinner with my family, I stay up a little bit later to research the passage that would have been Grandma Mimi's Torah portion.

Korach.

Numbers 16:1–16:32

Vayikach Korach ben-Yitshar   Korach, son of Yitz'har
ben-Kehat   grandson of Kehoth
ben-Levi veDatan va'Aviram   great-grandson of Levi,
beney Eli'av ve'On ben-Pelet   began a rebellion with
beney Re-uven   the descendants of Reuben

. . .

Vayikahalu al-Moshe   They went against Moses
ve'al-Aharon vayomeru   and Aaron and declared
alehem rav-lachem ki   to them, "You have gone
chol-ha'edah kulam   too far! All the people in
kedoshim uvetocham   the community are holy
Adonay umadua   and God is with them.
titnase'u al-kehal   Why do you put yourself
Adonay   above God's people?"

. . .

Vayedaber Adonay el-Moshe   God spoke to Moses
ve'el-Aharon lemor.   and Aaron, saying,
Hibadelu mitoch ha'edah   "Separate yourselves from
hazot va'achaleh otam   this community, and I will
keraga.   destroy them."

. . .

Vatiftach ha'arets et-piha   The earth opened its

vativla otam ve'et-bateyhem   mouth and swallowed

ve'et kol-ha'adam asher   them and their houses,

le-Korach ve'et   along with Korach's men

kol-harechush.   and their property.

Tikkun Olam

Grandma Mimi's Torah portion is called *Korach,* and once I find it, I read the English translation through once, front to back. And as soon as I'm done reading, I start over. Then I read it again. And again. And again. Soon I've read it more than a dozen times.

It's strange. Even though I'm exhausted and I've had a long day, I want to keep reading.

Korach is weird.

It's dark.

It's so *interesting.*

See, Korach is mad at Moses, and Moses is mad at Korach, but Moses has God on his side, and so God decides to punish Korach by opening a crack in the earth and swallowing him in it.

Which . . . seems kinda excessive, right?

Okay, maybe Korach was in the wrong. But does that give God the right to swallow people in the earth?

I guess it's silly to talk about rights when it comes to God. Whether you believe in God or not, it's canon that God can do whatever God wants.

But does this mean swallowing up people who hurt you is good?

Korach is human, and humans make mistakes, but don't humans also learn from those mistakes? Sometimes humans apologize. And grow. And fix the hurt they've caused. But if God swallows them up before they have a chance to fix that hurt, what a waste!

And by the way, since when is rebelling against authority such a bad thing? I mean, God comes from up high and is like, *Hi, obey me now!* and everyone is supposed to listen no matter what?

What if God is wrong?

What if God doesn't know you the way you know yourself, and when God asks you to do something that doesn't feel right, or tells you *not* to do something that *does* feel right, and you ignore God, is God going to swallow you up in the earth too, so you're not a problem anymore?

And while we're on the subject of swallowing people up, is there now a giant crack in the earth? Some gaping hole dividing the world in half as a reminder to never question God's authority?

Someone could be walking around, daydreaming about, I dunno, inventing the wheel—or whatever ancient Jews used to daydream about, and—WHAM!

Swallowed!

Who heals the earth when God is the one who broke it in the first place?

And what if someone else crosses God before people have time to fix earth's first hole, and now there are two holes? Three holes? Four?

At some point, is the earth going to be covered in gaps and cracks and holes, and no matter how much we try, it will never go back to the way it was?

Are we okay with that?

Well, I'm not!

I don't want the earth to be divided in half

and half again

and half again

until everyone is split into their own tiny square of humanity, until everyone is sitting alone in their bedroom at two a.m., having not spoken to any of their friends in months because they're too afraid to apologize, too afraid to forgive, too afraid to grow?

What if everyone did that?

What if any time anyone hurt anybody else, that person was swallowed up in the earth?

If everyone did that, eventually we'd all be alone.

If I keep doing that, I'll always be alone.

I don't want to be alone.

I'm tired of being alone.

I'd rather make amends than be alone.

Because mistakes are normal. Even the best bakers make mistakes in dishes they've made a million times. Grandma Mimi used to say any old schmuck can follow a recipe, but what separates a good baker from a great baker are the mistakes.

Maybe that's what separates a good friend from a great friend, too.

You forget to add the salt, you spray flour everywhere when your mixer jolts on, you accidentally add egg whites when you meant to add yolks, so maybe you double the recipe. Maybe you thicken the dough with flour. Maybe you thought you were making an angel food cake, but now you're making a yellow cake.

Food is salvageable. It's meant to be fun. And if you mess up, you fix it, or you try again tomorrow when you're a better baker.

Or a better human.

Why is that so hard when it comes to friendships?

Well, I'm tired of it.

I'm tired of losing my friends in the cracks in the earth.

I'm tired of giving up when it gets hard.
I'm tired of the fighting
and the lying
and the grudges.

If Sam and Dad can heal their earth, maybe it's time I heal mine.

So sound the shofar! Yom Kippur is coming early this year.

It's time to get my *tikkun olam* on.

Recipe for a New Start

Mix together
one (1) Big Book of What's Cooking
one (1) recipe for macaroons
one (1) smell of springtime
    because I'm starting to realize
    I've got to heal my own cracks in the earth.

Dear Aunt Yael,

April 11, 2:41 a.m.

I looked up what Torah portion Grandma Mimi would have had when she was a kid, and as it turns out, it would have been Korach.

So I wanted to say, although I think you did some things wrong, I don't want you to get swallowed up in the earth. I think I'd miss you.

Sincerely,

Hannah Malfa-Adler

Dear Hannah

April 11, 6:02 a.m.

I don't want you to get swallowed up in the earth, either :)

Love,

Aunt Yael

Back Home

It starts with a Tupperware full of macaroons and a long walk.

Past the house with the garden—purple flowers this time—through the yard of the house with all the construction —they're adding another bedroom now—and past the house with the used-to-be-yellow door.

I try not to look at it.

But eventually I'm in front of the house where I learned to build a fort. Where I set up my first lemonade stand. Where I once spent three days straight playing an extra-long game of Monopoly.

Shira's house.

I ring her doorbell, switching the Tupperware from one hand to the other until Shira answers.

"Hey, Hannah," she says.

It's weird seeing her this close after so many months of avoiding her. I don't recognize any of the clothes she's wearing, and she's taller than I remember. Even her face looks different. Older, maybe. Like she's also done some growing up. "Hey," I say. "Macaroon?"

I hand her the open Tupperware, and she takes one. She bites into it, and I take a deep breath to prepare myself before I say, "I'm here to apologize."

Recipe for an Apology

Mix together:

One (1) part acknowledging what you did wrong.

"You were right, Shira. Way back when I first said I was having a bat mitzvah, I was lying to you. I was lying to everybody. I said I was having a bat mitzvah because I felt like I needed to keep up with you. I was jealous, and I took that out on you."

One (1) part actually feeling bad about it.

"I feel awful. It was your big day, and you'd spent so much time practicing for it, and I made the whole thing about me. And you were right. I'd never cared about it before you had yours. I'd never been to temple with you or asked you about what you did at Hebrew school. And I'm *still* not sure if I believe in God.

"I didn't care about any of it until you were getting attention for it. It must have hurt to see the person you thought was your best friend trying to take such a big day from you."

One (1) part trying to fix the damage.

"I know I can't take back what I said, but I know now how much being Jewish must mean to you. How much it must have hurt to see me turning it into something small.

"I get it now. Sort of, anyway. I guess I still don't fully know what it means to be Jewish, but I know that to you at least, it means a lot. And I was trying to diminish that.

"I *am* Jewish, and when you said I wasn't, that hurt. But now I think I see what you meant.

"Being Jewish does matter to me now, but probably not in the same way it matters to you. And that's okay. I don't need to be Jewish the same way as you are. I don't need to be Jewish like anybody else.

"I need to be Jewish like me."

Best Friends

"I guess I'll leave now," I say. "I know you don't owe me forgiveness, so you don't have to do anything. Enjoy the macaroons, okay?" I set the Tupperware by Shira's feet and turn to walk back to my house.

But before I get down the stairs, Shira says, "I'm sorry, too."

I turn around to face her, not sure if I heard her right.

She walks across the front porch until she's standing next to me. Until she's so close I can smell her shampoo, count the freckles on her nose. So close she could hug me if she wanted to.

And then she does.

She squeezes me so tight it feels like a hundred hugs in one. Like months and months of hugs that were lost, that we can never get back, but maybe, if we squeeze each other tight enough right now, we might come close.

And when we finally let go, she says, "I never should have said you weren't really Jewish. That wasn't fair of me at all. It's not my decision to say what you are. And also, not that you need me to tell you at this point, but you clearly *are* Jewish."

I blink at Shira once, twice, three times. This is all I've ever wanted from her, to hug me and to tell me I'm Jewish, but now that I'm getting it, all I feel is confused. "What makes you say that?"

Shira laughs. "Do you know how much I fought my parents about going to Hebrew school? I used to pretend I was sick. Or I had too much homework. One time, after they dropped me off, I snuck out. And studying for my bat mitzvah was miserable! My parents had to literally sit next to me while I studied or I wouldn't have done it. If they had given me permission to quit at any point along the way, I think I would have."

"I didn't know that," I say.

Shira shrugs. "You didn't ask."

And she's right. I didn't ask. But I won't make that mistake again.

"My parents forced me to do everything involved with having a bat mitzvah, but no one was forcing you to study with your aunt. No one even wanted you to. I feel like that's more important than learning Hebrew. Wanting to learn it."

"Wait . . ." None of this is making sense right now. I feel like I'm in some sort of alternate reality. "I'm confused," I say. "Being Jewish means so much to you. And I was such a jerk about it!"

"Being Jewish does mean a lot to me," Shira says with a shrug. "But that doesn't mean I like every single part of it. And you *were* a jerk. But I was a jerk too. I was letting the attention from my bat mitzvah go to my head. And as soon as people stopped caring about it, I realized how stupid I was to want a break from you. I missed you. But you seemed to be having so much fun with your new friend, and it felt like this whole thing had gone on for so long that you didn't want anything to do with me anymore. At your grandma's shiva, I was waiting in your bedroom to tell you I was going to forgive you for lying about your bat mitzvah. I was so sure you had never been preparing anything, but when I heard you and your aunt fighting, I realized I was wrong all along. This whole time you *were* studying for your bat mitzvah, just like you told me, and I refused to believe you. I wanted to apologize right then, but you were so upset, and I was kind of shocked, I guess. And really, I . . . I guess I was scared."

My mouth is numb. Maybe a magic genie did grant me my wish and somehow we've gone back to September. But it's not September. It's April, and it's springtime, and Shira is apologizing to *me*.

"Thank you," I finally say. And it feels too small to be a good response, but I can't find better words, so I say it again. "Thank you."

We stand in silence after that. Like the awkward pause that happens at the end of a big meal, where everyone has run out of things to talk about but nobody wants to leave the safety of the table, so you sit and stare at each other, tongue-tied. Full, happy, enjoying the in-between.

Eventually I look at the Tupperware resting on the steps and I pick it up. "Another macaroon?" I ask.

She takes one, bites into it, and says, "Always."

Recipe for Forgiveness

Mix together
two (2) girls
    who
            have seen *Finding Nemo*
            forty-one (41) — no, forty-two (42) — times
    who
            have built more blanket forts
            than they can remember
    who
            learned to read in daycare
            by reading aloud
            to each other
    who
            have spent the past six (6) months
            pretending the other
            didn't exist.

Add in
one (1) day spent
    playing board games
    baking Forgiveness Fudge
    and catching each other up

on everything that happened
since they stopped talking.

Mix in
one (1) invitation
   at the end of the day
   for a bat mitzvah
   that should have happened
   sixty-four (64) years ago.

Bake for ten (10) seconds
in the April sunset
   (approximately 52 degrees)
and you'll get
one (1)
   "Yes! I'll be there! I wouldn't miss it for the
   world!"
and two (2)
best friends
   maybe not quite back to normal
   but pretty darn close.

A Second Attempt at Apologies

Soufflés are a tricky sort of dish.

If you contaminate your egg whites with just the tiniest bit of yolk, the soufflés won't rise in the oven. If you don't fold the whites delicately into the batter, the soufflés will collapse. If your oven is too hot in some patches or too cold in others, if it's wetter outside than you were expecting, or if you're used to making soufflés in summer and you try making them in winter, they will turn out so poorly, you'll wonder why you didn't stick with something simple.

Soufflés are hard. They can turn out perfectly in the morning, but if you try them again that very same day, you might end up with egg on your face.

Kind of like apologies.

I walk to Vee's house next, a second Tupperware full of peace-offering macaroons in my hands. And I'm feeling good this time. This time, my apology recipe is tried-and-true.

I ring Vee's doorbell, and right away things don't feel right. I was expecting Vee to answer the door, like Shira answered the door at her house. But it's not Vee who answers, it's her mom. Ezter.

"Hi," I say. "Is Vee here?" I show her the Tupperware full of macaroons, but Ezter doesn't look impressed. I hadn't thought about it, but I wonder if Vee told her family the real reason I left their house that day.

Ezter looks at her watch. "Do you realize how late it is?" she asks. And I guess I hadn't thought about that either, since the plan was always to go to Shira's first, then go to Vee's. But I stayed longer at Shira's than I meant to, and from the sounds and smells of what is going on in Vee's house, I've interrupted dinner.

"I'm sorry," I say, scrunching up my face. "I can come back later. Tomorrow, I mean. Or next weekend."

But then Vee arrives and gently nudges Ezter out of the way. "It's fine," she says to her stepmom—I mean, mom—who doesn't look convinced. "Really," Vee repeats. "It's okay. I'll clear the dishes in a minute."

Ezter shakes her head and walks down the hallway.

"Hey," I say, suddenly feeling awkward. "I haven't seen you around much lately."

Vee bites her lip. "That was intentional."

"I know," I say. I kick a piece of gravel, trying to find something to say. "I keep seeing you in the orchestra room at lunch. Does that mean you're playing flute?"

Vee shrugs.

"I think I heard you playing once," I continue. "A few months ago. You're really good."

"So are you here to apologize, or what?"

"Oh, right," I say, shaking my head and handing her the Tupperware. "These are for you." Vee takes them, but she doesn't open them. She holds the macaroons close to her chest and waits for me to get on with it.

"Okay." I clasp my hands together. "I wanted to apologize for what I said at your house that day. That you weren't really Jewish. You were right when you said I believed it, because I did believe it. It's what I'd been taught, but I guess I hadn't thought about what it meant. And when I did think about it, I realized it didn't make sense. Instead of defending myself, I should have listened to you when you said I was wrong. I'm working on being better at that."

Vee's posture relaxes. "Go on," she says, and my lips can't help but curl into a cautious smile. Maybe this is going to work, after all.

"I feel horrible about the whole thing," I continue. "Because I know how much it hurts when people don't see you the way you see yourself. People have been doing that with me my whole life, and I can't believe I made someone else feel as bad as other people have made me feel."

Vee is nodding now, and her arms drop from in front of her chest.

"But more than that," I continue, "I saw what someone did to your house. What someone did to you. And every time I thought about it, I remembered something my grandmother said to me. We don't let people who hate us decide who we are. And I kept thinking how unfair it was that you got it from both sides. One day I could say you weren't Jewish enough, and the next, someone else could say you were too Jewish. And every time I saw your door and how it used to be yellow but now was black, it hurt as much as it did that first day. And I wanted someone to do something about it. To figure out who did it or promise it wouldn't happen again, but no one could promise me that, so I didn't know what to do. I pretended it didn't happen and felt sick to my stomach every time I thought about it. I guess I see what you meant now — about hate.

"I also realized something. It's probably easier *not* to be Jewish. Especially in a world where someone can paint something like that on your door and get away with it. So if you choose to be Jewish when you don't have to, it might mean even more to you than to people who don't have a choice."

Vee is quiet now, as if she's thinking things over, and I'm about ready to begin the third ingredient of my apology, trying to make things right, when she jumps in. "Do you know why I hide my necklace?" she asks.

I pause. This wasn't part of my recipe. "Because of people like that?" I ask. "People who paint horrible things on doors?"

Vee wobbles her head back and forth. "Sort of," she says. "When I wear my necklace on the outside of my shirt, people look at me funny. I get stupid questions and stupid looks, and sometimes people say mean things. Sometimes they mean to be mean, and sometimes they don't, but it hurts either way."

"Like when I said you weren't really Jewish."

"Yes," Vee says. "And?"

I shake my head. "And . . ."

"And . . . if someone learns I'm Jewish and their response is, 'But you're Spanish?'"

"Wait . . ." It takes me a minute to remember, but when I do, it feels like I've been punched in the gut. "Vee . . . That was me. *I* said that to you."

Vee makes a sound like a laugh, but it sure doesn't feel like one. "Look, it's not only you. You were just the one I decided to keep trying with."

I'm not sure what to say to that. Part of me is flattered that she wanted to keep trying with me, but as soon as I let myself feel good, a whole new wave of bad hits me, because I ruined everything by saying what I said. Maybe Vee shouldn't have kept trying with me.

"I'm sorry," I say again. And I wish those words could hold all that I'm feeling.

"Look," Vee continues. "I appreciate that you were angry when our house got hit. It made me angry too."

"Yeah," I say. "I was sad not to see you in school that day. I wanted to make sure you were okay."

For some reason Vee seems amused by this. She laughs once and then grows quiet again. "Do you understand why I wasn't in school that day?"

"Because you were scared," I say. "Because it was safer at home." But as I say it, I realize that answer doesn't quite make sense. The person had vandalized her home. Wouldn't she have been safer *out* of her home?

Vee shakes her head. "My parents didn't want me to go to school that day. They thought there was a chance that whoever did it went to school with me. I look different from a lot of the other students there. I stick out, Hannah, and my parents thought that maybe some people at school don't like it. They worried that if I went, I might actually be closer to the person who tagged our house than if I stayed home. The person could have been someone I see every day. Someone who was mad at me for some reason. Maybe even someone I thought was a friend."

She pauses here and gives me a moment to put the pieces together. And when I do, my heart sinks.

When all this happened, Vee's only friend in school was . . . *me*.

"Wait . . ." I say. "Vee . . . you didn't think *I* painted that symbol on your door. Did you?"

Vee shakes her head. "Of course not. I know you wouldn't do that."

But something about the way she says this makes me wonder if the thought didn't at least cross her mind.

"I didn't do it," I say. "I swear I didn't."

"I know that." She crosses her arms back over her chest. "Seriously. I know."

I feel sick to my stomach now, in a way I didn't expect coming into this. In a way I couldn't have anticipated until I was looking at Vee face to face. This whole time I've felt like whoever painted the symbol on Vee's door might as well have painted it on mine too. That's how much it hurt. But the third ingredient in an apology is undoing the damage I caused. I know I wasn't the one who painted her door, and I know Vee knows it, too, but right now that doesn't feel like enough.

"I'm so sorry," I say again, but it feels pitiful coming out of my mouth.

"Thanks." Vee shrugs. "I appreciate you coming over here. Really." She shakes the Tupperware and says, "Thanks for this, too. Damien will go bananas for them. And I appreciate the apology." She quirks the left side of her mouth up. "You're getting better at them."

She starts to close the door, but before she does, I stop her. "Vee?" I ask.

"Yeah?"

"How many days left?"

Vee looks at me for a moment, confused, but then recognition hits her. "Fifty-eight," she says, and closes the door.

I'm left staring at the blackness.

A Third Attempt at Apologies

It's weird how easily things slip back to normal after that. At least some version of normal.

Shira and I sit together on the bus now, along with Jeremy Brewer, of course. Shira doesn't flip her hair at him anymore, and she's eased off the makeup, but she's still wearing dresses now that it's warm out. Jeremy's talking more than he did at the beginning, and he's actually kind of funny now that I'm giving him a chance.

I guess it's not so terrible that Shira's dating him.

I sit with my old table at lunch again, too. Everyone is talking about how Lin is going to try out for the soccer team in the fall, and how Chris W. has a solo in the spring band concert, but he's so nervous, he's wishing he'd never auditioned.

And it's nice. Being back at my old table, as if nothing ever happened. But it's kind of like going back to your favorite recipe after not eating it for a year. When you go back, it tastes the same, but you've changed.

It's great being friends with Shira again. It feels comfortable, but I miss Vee. I hate not knowing where we stand.

"I can't stop thinking about it," I tell Shira and Jeremy on the bus home from school one day. "I can't stop thinking about why someone would do that to her just because she's Jewish."

"Wait," says Shira. "Victoria is Jewish? I thought she was from Brazil or something."

"Her family is from Guatemala," I say. "And the two aren't mutually exclusive."

"Oh," says Shira. "I didn't know that. Thanks for telling me."

I sigh. "I just wish I could catch whoever did it. I wish I could go back in time and put a camera in front of Vee's house. Or a booby trap on her porch."

"Nah," says Jeremy. "Even if you caught the guy, it wouldn't matter."

"What do you mean?" I say. "Of course it would matter. They should pay for what they did."

"But catching them doesn't fix the problem. This isn't, like, Scooby-Doo or whatever. If it wasn't that guy, it'd be some other guy." Jeremy picks at his backpack strap. "It sucks, but there's nothing we can do about it."

"Well, that's pessimistic."

"It's the way it is."

I look to Shira, hoping she'll have something positive to say about this whole thing, but she's scrunching her nose up, like she agrees with Jeremy. "Sorry, Hannah," she says. "That happens at Beth Shalom all the time. I don't know if we ever find out who did it. We just wash it off or paint over it and pretend it was never there."

"But how can you pretend it was never there?" I ask. "Doesn't it bother you?"

"Of course it does," Shira says, her voice getting quiet. "But if I think about it too much, it becomes all I think about."

"Yeah," I say. "It's awful." And it is, but *awful* feels like too small a word. Any word would feel like too small a word. Horrible. Terrible. Unfair. How can people cause so much hurt and get away with it?

Jeremy and Shira get off at the next stop, and I'm left on the bus as it drives by Vee's door, still painted black.

I hate it. It feels like it's stuck in mourning clothes. Like it's in a permanent shiva. I wish I could unpaint it, or repaint it.

Vee was my friend, and I should have helped her.

So, instead of getting off at my usual stop, I get off early. I send a text to my parents that I'm going to be home a little late, and I hop on another bus to head to the nearest hardware store, where I pick up three things: a card, a paintbrush, and a can of yellow paint.

Dear Vee,

Just in case you ever want to bring back the
sunshine.

Love,
Hannah.

P.S. We both guessed wrong: it wasn't the hair
tie thing OR the pescacide thing.

P.P.S. I'm having a bat mitzvah for Grandma Mimi
this summer. June 10th, at 7:30 p.m. I understand if you don't want to come, or if you're
back in Miami by then, but I figured I'd invite
you anyway, since I'd love to see you there.

P.P.P.S. I hope you don't actually move back to
Miami. I would miss you. I hope we get to hang
out this summer.

Summer

Summer

Summer is when we make passion fruit ice cream.

"In honor of the last day of school and the start of bat mitzvah planning!" I say, and Shira lifts her spoon in agreement.

"Here, here!" we say at the same time.

The house is hot and sticky because our air conditioner's been on the fritz, so nothing is more welcoming than coming into a kitchen that smells like cream and citrus with a hint of lime zest.

It's so good that I go back to the freezer for seconds.

"Save some for next week," Sam says, arm-deep in soapy sink water. "You think I've been working this hard just so you and Shira could pig out?"

Shira makes an oink sound from the kitchen table, and I make one too.

"You really are a pair of freaks," Sam says, and Shira and I laugh so hard we choke on our ice cream.

It's good to have her back.

Sam's barely been out of school for a week, and already he's preparing for Grandma Mimi's bat mitzvah. He claims it's to stay in shape for National Hobart's pre-freshman program, which starts in August, but I know that's just an excuse. And anyway, I don't care. I'll take any excuse I can get for passion fruit ice cream.

The bat mitzvah is going to be exactly what she would have wanted: a Shabbat dinner and small ceremony around a dinner table filled with her favorite people and covered with so much food we'll have to roll ourselves to bed that night.

Even Mom and Dad are excited. Last night I caught Dad leafing through the Big Book of What's Cooking and flagging his favorite recipes. And ever since Grandma Mimi's shiva, Mom doesn't seem as reluctant to do Jewish stuff as she once did. She even helped me find the Shabbat candles in the attic. And whenever we mention that this would have been Grandma Mimi's seventy-seventh birthday, she gets all teary-eyed.

It feels good to go into this with a team. Not sneaking behind everyone's back, but being able to talk about it with the people who mean the most to me. To plan the menu with Sam and get a ride from Dad to the grocery store. To go to the farmers' market with Shira, since they have the best eggs and berries, and be able to talk about logistics with Mom.

The only thing missing in this whole thing is Vee, but I haven't spoken to her since I tried to apologize. Well, except for when I congratulated her, Maggie Sakurai, and Kwame James on their flute trio performance at the spring band concert. Vee smiled at me and said thanks, and that was the end of it. And now that school is finished and her countdown clock has run out, I don't know if she's even living here anymore.

I walk past her house once that week, looking for moving vans, listening for flute music, but I don't hear or see anything. I even force myself to look at her door, in hopes that maybe there's a summer wreath hanging on it, or maybe she'll have used the yellow paint I gave her. But there's no wreath, and the door is as black as ever.

I remind myself that it's okay. I tried my best, and Vee doesn't have to forgive me if she doesn't want to. Usually I believe this, because if Vee moves back to Miami, she'll be happy. She'll play the flute in the house where her birth mom used to live, and she'll be warm all year round. In the meantime, I busy myself with plans for Grandma Mimi's bat mitzvah. With that, at least, I know one hundred percent for sure I'm doing the right thing.

~~Pasion~~ Passion Fruit Ice Cream

1 1/2C sugar

3 eggs

3C heavy cream

1 1/2C passion fruit pulp

Whisk sugar and eggs and boil cream. Add cream to eggs.
Pour into saucepan and cook. Sieve mixture and add pulp.
Chill and add mixture to ice cream machine.

But don't
let the eggs
curdle!

Remember:

The sourer the winter

the sweeter the summer.

The Menu

For the main meal,
we will have brisket and potato latkes and
a spinach salad.
Simple.
Easy.
I would even say
minimalist.

But for dessert?
All of Grandma Mimi's favorites.
Special-occasion treats
holiday desserts
just-because-we-wanted-to snacks,
but everything has one common ingredient:
Grandma Mimi.

Rugelach and
apple walnut pie and
chocolate chocolate chunk cookies and
buttermilk biscuits and
challah and
sufganiyot and

chocolate chip pancakes and
baklava and
macaroons and
passion fruit ice cream and
a million more things, besides

and last but not least
her cake.

Babka

For the dough:

    3 3/4C flour

    1/2C sugar

    1T yeast

    cinnamon to taste

    3 eggs

    1/2C water

    big pinch of salt

    2/3C butter ← SOFTENED!

For the chocolate:

    1/2C powdered sugar

    1/3C cocoa powder

    1 bar of melted dark chocolate

    1/2C melted butter

    chocolate chips to taste

Whisk flour, sugar, yeast, and cinnamon; add eggs and water until it forms a dough. Add salt and butter bit by bit and mix until dough feels like chewing gum in your hands. Rise dough overnight. ← oiled bowl, in the fridge

Mix filling ~~ingreden~~ ingredients together and spread on rolled-out dough, sprinkle with chocolate chips to taste, then fold into a loaf.

Bake in oven at 375 until it passes the toothpick test.

Brush with a simple syrup while warm.

Remember:

Babka means grandmother

because it takes a lifetime to master.

Brack to Brormal Brownies

"What should we call these now?" asks Shira.

With just one day to go until the bat mitzvah, it's all hands on deck. Mom and Dad are cleaning the house while Sam and Shira help me in the kitchen. Sam's folding hamantaschen dough into triangles while Shira and I pop a batch of our famous Jeremy Brewer Brownies into the oven.

"Yeah," I say. "It feels weird to call them Jeremy Brewer Brownies now."

"How about Back to Normal Brownies?" she asks.

"How about Brack to Brormal Brownies?" I say, and Shira laughs.

"I like that," she says. "Brack to Brormal Brownies."

I stick my finger into the bowl and lick the raw batter off my finger. "Brelicious," I say.

"Bragnificent!"

"Brarvelous!"

She snorts. "You have chocolate all over your face."

I take the spatula and smear it across my cheek. "Bretter?"

"Bretter."

"Hey, weirdos," Sam calls from across the room. "Can you come over here and check this out? I can't get the filling to stop leaking out the edges."

"What's wrong?" Shira and I walk over to see what Sam needs, licking chocolate off our faces as we go, but when I get there, all the hamantaschen are perfectly folded on a sheet pan.

When I realize what's about to happen, it's too late, and both Shira and I have fistfuls of sugar in our hair.

"Hey!" I grab Sam's hands while Shira grabs a fistful of sugar from the sack and pours it directly on Sam's head.

"Argh!" Sam shouts. "This was a lot more fun when you two were short."

Then he's laughing, which means I'm laughing, which means Shira is laughing, and if any of us had any worries remaining, we don't anymore. They all have melted away, like butter in a hot oven.

One Last Hole in the Earth

It's the night before the party, and everything is ready to go. The food is prepared, my outfit is picked out, I've learned the first few lines of *Korach,* and there's nothing more on my to-do list.

But I can't shake the feeling that I've forgotten to add salt to the piecrust.

Something is missing, and I think I know what it is.

"Hey Mom?" I ask. "I have a question. About tomorrow."

Mom looks up at me from the stack of papers she's grading. You'd think her work would lighten up now that it's summer, but she actually takes on more classes during summer break than during the school year.

"I was thinking," I say, "about the guest list. And who's on it and who's not, and I was wondering if maybe you thought we should invite Aunt Yael?"

Mom clicks her pen closed.

"I know you're mad at her still," I continue, "and I haven't forgotten about what happened either, but I do believe she's changed, and I'm wondering if maybe it's time we tried to stop being mad?"

I think about how sometimes the best relationships need a break, a sabbatical year, like the land in *Behar.* Aunt Yael once said that relationships are living, breathing ecosystems, and if we let them rest, they can come back one day, stronger than ever.

But that only works if, eventually, the sabbatical ends.

"I think the reason," I continue, choosing my words carefully, "Grandma Mimi took me to study with Aunt Yael is so she would have a chance to undo what she did. And if you saw she was sorry, maybe you would forgive her."

I pause, waiting for my words to sink in. Maybe reminding Mom of Grandma Mimi will remind her of a family in one piece. Of baking biscuits in the kitchen with her sister and slathering them with watermelon jelly.

Maybe.

"Hannah," Mom says. "Haven't we had this conversation before?"

"Not in the last few days."

"But what did I say last time?"

I wish Mom didn't make me reject myself. "You said no."

"I said no." Mom clicks her pen open and closed, open and closed. "So what do you think I'm going to say this time?"

Mom doesn't wait for me to respond. She turns around and goes back to grading, as if I'm not here.

Practicing

That night, for what may be the last time ever, I practice my Torah portion.

Or rather, I practice Grandma Mimi's Torah portion.

I play the recording I found online, and I whisper-sing the words the way I did back when I was studying *Behar* in secret.

I guess I don't need to whisper-sing anymore, since everyone knows what I'm doing, but I like to whisper-sing. It makes me feel like I'm doing this just for me and Grandma Mimi. Like these words belong to us and us alone, even though I know they've been sung by thousands of people in the past and will be sung by thousands more in the future.

Tonight, they're just ours.

The Missing Ingredient

By the time my eyes are drooping, the house is dark and silent, and it seems like I'm the only one awake.

Which is why, once I've brushed my teeth and tucked myself into bed, I'm surprised to hear someone knock on my bedroom door.

"Come in," I say, expecting my night-owl brother with a burning question about the flavor profile of a sweet potato pie. Or my mom, anxious about tomorrow, asking me if I'm *certain* I don't want to start dinner just a tad on the early side.

But when the door creaks open, I know before I turn on my lamp it's neither Mom nor Sam.

"Dad?" I ask. "Are you okay? Why aren't you asleep?"

"Everything's fine," Dad whispers, putting his finger to his lips, as if we're going to wake up the house if we aren't careful. "You weren't asleep, were you?"

I shake my head. "What's up?"

Dad doesn't answer right away, and if I didn't know better, I would say he seems nervous. "I have something you might want," he says finally. "She's kept it in a drawer all these years. I think she thinks she threw it away, but . . ." he holds out his fist, clutching some mysterious object. "I think you should have it for tomorrow."

Once it's in my hand, I'm still not sure what it's supposed to be. It's soft and worn, and when I take the whatever-it-is into the lamplight, all I see is a ball of yellow notepad paper.

But before I have a chance to unfold it, Dad says something under his breath, so quietly I can barely hear him.

"What's that?" I say.

Dad sighs, and in the dim light he looks embarrassed, as if he's going to say, *Forget it, go back to sleep,* but he doesn't. Instead he says, "You know all we want is what's best for you, right? For you and your brother. Sometimes your mom and I don't make the right calls, but I promise, all we want is what's best for you two."

I nod. I'm not sure what else to do, and when he doesn't say any more, I say, "I know that."

Dad shoves his hands into his pajama pockets and nods at the wad of paper in my hands. "I know it's late, but I think there's still time to make a batch before dinner tomorrow."

And with that, he heads back down the hallway toward his own room, leaving me alone.

I slowly unroll the paper and see what he wanted me to have.

In two different little-girl handwritings, on paper that looks like it was torn out of the Big Book of What's Cooking, is a recipe I've never seen before.

~~Wattermelon~~ Watermelon Jelly

4 cups watermelon ← pureed

roasted jalapenos to desired heat,
    peeled

4t pecktin powder

1/4c sugar

pinch of salt

2 limes

parsley

lemon zest

Drain watermelon over cheesecloth. Place
    liquid in sauce pan. Add lime juice, sugar, salt.
    Then boil. Remove seeds from ~~jalapenyos,~~ jalapenos
    chop, and add to boiling mixture. Add pecktin
    and boil further. Add chopped parsley and
    lemon zest. When ready, put in jars and
    soak in water bath. Cool until ready to
    serve.

Remember:

The spicy is important
in the midst of the sweet.

Yael is
sorry she
can't spell!

At least she
can cook!

Sweet and Spicy

As soon as Mom leaves to teach her early-morning summer school class the next day, I make a last-minute run to the store to buy the final ingredients for Grandma Mimi's perfect bat mitzvah.

Natural

It's an hour away.

After so many days of preparation, it's finally happening.

It's three in the afternoon. Shira's here already, dressed in her Shabbat best and helping me get ready for the big day, and I'm running out of tasks to check off from my to-do list.

Finally I have a minute to breathe. I shower, get dressed, and heat up my hair straightener. I've gotten good at this after doing it so much this year. Mom even bought me a spray bottle last week to keep my hair from frizzing in the summer humidity.

No one would ever know I have curly hair.

I pull out a single curl from in front of my right ear. I open the mouth of the iron and clasp it around the curl and—

—I stop.

I set the straightener down and look at the curl in the mirror.

It's kind of cool how it dried today, sort of like a rotini noodle, except a bit less cookie-cutter. It curls one way at the top and another way at the bottom, and it looks like what it might look like if I got my hair curled in one of those fancy salons.

Except I didn't go to a salon.

This is how my hair looks.

I separate another lock of hair and study that one in the mirror. And the more I look at that curl, the more I want to look at the next one, and the next one.

This one zigs left

and zags right

and this one zags right

and zigs left

and this one doesn't zag at all   it zigs

and this one, randomly, is totally straight and soft

and before I know it, fifteen minutes have gone by, and at this point I don't have enough time to

tame

calm

buff

shine

flatten straight

my f r i z z y

lint ball

dust bunny

cotton candy

hair.

Even if I wanted to.

Recipe for Grandma Mimi's Bat Mitzvah

Mix together
four (4) guests
    Sam
    Mom
    Dad
    Shira
at least a hundred (100) hours of cooking
    twenty-three (23) different foods
one (1) bright blue spaghetti strap dress
and one (1) necklace
    pulled from a box
    up in the attic
    sitting warm
    around my neck.

A Gift

It feels weird to be wearing it, like putting on someone else's shoes, but today, of all days, I want the necklace to be seen.

The party should be starting soon, since all the guests are already at our house, so any minute now, Grandma Mimi's bat mitzvah is going to begin.

Mom meets me at the stairs and asks, "You ready?"

"I'm ready," I say, adjusting the necklace so the star sits right in the center of my chest.

"Wait." She stops in her tracks. "What's that?"

I graze my fingers against the necklace. "Grandma Mimi gave it to me," I say. "She said it was yours when you were little. But she found it in the attic a while back and thought I might want it."

I say this like it's no big deal, but Mom is . . .

. . . well . . .

. . . Mom doesn't look so great.

"I thought it was gone," she says, her voice wet and wobbly. "I hadn't seen it in ages. Did my mom have it this whole time?"

"I . . . I don't know . . ." I say. "She *just* gave it to me this past Christmas. Well . . . this past Hanukkah."

Mom doesn't seem to hear me. "I took it off when I was packing my dad's boxes," she says. "After he died. I thought it must have . . ." She steadies herself on the banister. "Or that Yael might have . . ."

She doesn't finish her sentence, and I'm not sure if she's waiting for me to respond. "Mom?" I say finally. "Do you want it?"

Mom lets go of the banister. "No! No. I couldn't take it from you. Grandma Mimi wanted you to have it." She puts her hand on my shoulder and squeezes.

But wearing the necklace has never felt quite right, so I unclip it from my neck and place it in the palm of my mother's hand. "No," I say. "She wanted *you* to have it."

Surprises

The doorbell rings.

"I've got it!" I say, and I run to the door. Dinner is starting any minute, and I'm not sure who could be coming to our house this late on a Friday night.

I pull open the door, expecting to see a delivery person or something, but it's not a delivery person at all.

It's Vee.

She's carrying a Tupperware and is dressed in the same ripped-up jeans she always is, but this time, instead of her usual hoodie, she's wearing a black tank top, with a delicate golden star necklace sitting proudly on her chest.

"Vee?" I ask. "What are you doing here? What's in the Tupperware? And why are you not back in Miami? And you're not wearing a hoodie!"

"Whoa!" says Vee. "Slow down. I don't know what *you're* doing here, but *I* was invited to a bat mitzvah. See?" She holds up the Tupperware. "I even brought buñuelos! You know, like sufganiyot, only better? And I clearly am not in Miami right now. I decided not to move back. Turns out I can't live in Miami *and* keep playing in my new flute trio. Plus, there's a *small chance* I would miss you if I left. SMALL!" She points her finger at me.

"And I'm not wearing a hoodie, because . . ." Her hand jumps to the gold star around her neck. "Because I figured maybe today I could see what it feels like not to hide it. You know?"

I scrunch my hair up. "Yeah. I do know."

Vee rolls her eyes, as if to undo the seriousness of our last words. "Besides, it's hot as a freaking oven outside today! Did you know that Chicago could get this hot in the summer? If you did, you probably should have told me."

My mouth hangs open, and I have nothing to say. I'm just so glad to see her.

"You going to invite me inside?" Vee says. "Because if you don't, I'm going to start eating buñuelos in front of you, and as you know, I charge a viewing fee."

But instead of moving aside so Vee can walk into my house, I throw my arms around her. "I'm so sorry," I mumble into her hair. "I'm so glad you're here. I'm so sorry."

"Gah!" Vee says. "You're choking me!"

"Sorry!" I say, letting her out of my hug.

"Hey," Vee says, suddenly all serious. "Lesson number three on apologies? Know when one is accepted."

I reach my hand out in a non-ironic high-five. "Deal."

Vee slaps it, but rolls her eyes. I'll take it.

"Hannah?" Shira calls my name from the kitchen. "Where did you go?"

I gesture for Vee to follow me into the kitchen, where Shira has been helping me. "Shira?" I say. "I want to introduce you to someone."

It's weird to think Shira and Vee haven't officially met each other, but I guess they never had the chance.

"Vee?" I say. "This is Shira. My best friend. And Shira? This is Vee." I smile. "My other best friend."

Spotlight

Six people sit around the Shabbat table — Me, Mom, Dad, Sam, Shira, and Vee — and in some ways, it's no different from any other Shabbat dinner I've ever had at Shira's house. But this time, as I wash my hands before the first part of the ceremony, I remember how, after Shira's bat mitzvah, she seemed older. As if she'd become an adult overnight. And even though I know it's impossible to go from kid to grownup in the span of a single evening, I do feel like maybe somewhere in the last year I grew up a bit.

Tonight, I'm the one who lights the Shabbat candles. I'm the one who pours the wine into the glasses. I'm the one who says the prayers, and I'm going to be the one to serve the food.

Tonight is my night to show what I've learned from Grandma Mimi.

Because of her.

With her.

Tonight is our night to shine.

Blessing Over the Wine

Baruch ata Adonai
Eloheinu
Melech ha-olam
boreh p'ri hagafen.
Ah-
ah-
mein!

Bat Mitzvah, Part I

The service has ended, and now is the time when, if this were any other Shabbat dinner, we would eat. But this isn't any other Shabbat dinner.

This is a bat mitzvah.

So I stand up, clear my throat, and talk.

"When Grandma Mimi was a kid, girls weren't allowed to have bat mitzvahs. But Grandma Mimi wanted one. She wanted it so much her teeth hurt, she told me. She wanted the party, sure, and the dancing, and the cake, but what she really wanted was to read from the Torah.

Well, she never got a chance to do that. So I figured tonight could be my way of giving her the bat mitzvah she always wanted. All her favorite foods are here, and all her favorite people as well. And—"

"Wait—"

A Mitzvah

"Wait," Mom says again, chewing on something I can't see. "All her favorite people aren't here."

And that's when I realize what she's eating. On her plate is a biscuit, browned to perfection, with a bite taken out of it. And resting beside her is a spoon covered with spicy watermelon jelly.

Recipe for a Reunion

Mix together
    one (1) phone call
    thirty (30) minutes of waiting
    one (1) doorbell ring.

Stir in
    one (1) "Hi" from Aunt Yael
    one (1) "Hey" from Mom
and bake for thirty (30) seconds
    in awkward silence
    but understand
    this is just the start.

Bat Mitzvah Part II

"Now that everyone is here," I start, looking out into the audience of my family and friends, "it's time for Grandma Mimi's Torah portion.

"*Korach*."

I take out my stapled-together speech and read what I prepared.

"Someone once told me that the Torah is a series of metaphors we can use to apply to our own lives. And parts of *Korach* are perfect metaphors for Grandma Mimi's life these past few years.

"Like the part where groups of people turned against each other, even though they were all supposed to be on the same team. Or the part where it became easier for everyone to let their enemies be swallowed up by the earth. Or the part where forgiveness was seen as weakness, and spite was seen as strength.

"When I first read *Korach*, it felt like a warning. Like it was a worst-case scenario for what happens if we forget we're all on the same team. If we try to force other people to believe in the same things as we do, we end up with a hole in the earth, and the people we once cared about get swallowed up in it.

"Well, Grandma Mimi didn't want to make holes in the earth. She wanted to help fix the holes that were already there.

"And she did heal the earth, even if she didn't live long enough to get to see the holes close up all the way.

"She spent her whole life trying to keep her family together, and I think that's what she was trying to do when she helped me prepare for my own bat mitzvah this past year.

"I know that ended up being a bust. I didn't want it for the right reasons, and I think it's good that it didn't end up happening. At least not the way I wanted it to. I know this is Grandma Mimi's bat mitzvah, not mine, but there's a part of me that feels like it *is* mine. Like, by sitting here with you all tonight, reciting Grandma Mimi's Torah portion for her, cooking all her favorite foods, I'm keeping something alive.

"Maybe that thing I'm keeping alive is religion. Or maybe it's family. Or maybe it's God. Or maybe it's the recipe for the best rugelach you've ever eaten in your life.

"I'm not sure what it is.

"But I think it's being Jewish.

"Choosing to keep that part of me alive even if it's easier, safer, to let it die.

"I spent a lot of time this year thinking I'm not really Jewish. And I know there are some people out there who still probably think that. Who even hate me for it. But there are also people who hate me for being *too* Jewish.

"So isn't it easier if I decide for myself?

"Well, I think I have. I'm Jewish. And Grandma Mimi would have liked that.

"So, in honor of her seventy-seventh birthday, I'm going to recite the Torah portion she never got a chance to.

"Korach."

Sheva

Sometimes, when you're baking something new, you look at the recipe and have a picture in your head of what it's going to look like, smell like, taste like—and it comes out of the oven nothing like you pictured.

I thought at my bat mitzvah I'd be seated beside Shira, but instead, Shira is on one side and Vee is on the other.

I thought my hair would shine bright and straight, but instead I let it curl its natural curl.

I thought we would dance the hora in a circle in a party room with a hired DJ, but instead we sit in a circle around the same dinner table we always do.

I thought I'd be lifted up in a chair by my friends and classmates, but I spend the meal on my butt, surrounded by the people who love me most.

Maybe my perfect bat mitzvah never happened, but not in my wildest dreams did I think I'd sit at a table with Sam and Dad, Mom and Aunt Yael, Vee and Shira all at once, no fighting, no shouting, just food and love.

And as I wash my hands before the dinner part of the ceremony, I realize something.

Today there are seven people around my dinner table.

Sheva

sheva

sheva.

And maybe Mom and Aunt Yael don't quite remember how to talk to each other.

And maybe Dad still makes some of his "just joking" jokes.

And maybe I made like a million mistakes while reciting the few lines of *Korach* I managed to learn in the last few weeks, since I didn't have Aunt Yael's help on it like I did with *Behar*.

But there are seven people eating a Shabbat dinner made out of all of Grandma Mimi's favorite foods.

And seven means luck.

Completion.

Holiness.

Seven means family.

Yellow

That night, Shira, Vee, and I paint a door.

It's late, and it's dark, and we're so full our stomachs hurt, but we do it anyway.

Because sometimes when the night is darkest, that's when we most need the sunshine.

Fall

Recipe for My Family

Mix together
one (1) Mom
    named Liat
    with big curly hair
    she always wears straight
    and a tarnished silver necklace
    she never takes off
one (1) Dad
    named Richard
    with a bald patch
    and a gap between his front teeth
    mostly okay with the fact that his son
    just left for culinary school
one (1) brother
    named Sam
    who grew up
    despite our best efforts
one (1) aunt
    named Yael
    who's back for good this time
one (1) best friend
    named Shira

who broke up with Jeremy

but still wears dresses

because she likes how they make her feel

one (1) best friend

called Vee

who plays flute in our school orchestra

and no longer

counts down

one (1) Grandma Mimi

who died

but isn't gone

and one (1) me

Hannah

who says things she doesn't mean

and means things she doesn't say

but eventually

hopefully

gets it right in the end.

Bake in Chicago

At -10 degrees in the winter

and 110 degrees in the summer

for the rest of the future

because a family is as dependable

as vanilla ice cream
and it will rise like a yeasted dough
no matter what happens
between one fall and the next.

Author's Note

Just like me, Hannah Malfa-Adler is Jew . . . ish.

Just like Hannah, I have a mom who was raised Jewish and a dad who was raised Catholic, but neither of our parents participate in any form of organized religion today.

We both have maternal grandmothers who identify strongly as Jewish and who believe their identities make us Jewish too.

We both have struggled with feeling comfortable calling ourselves Jewish, and both Hannah and I, at one point or another, have wondered if we even want to be Jewish at all.

To top it all off, both Hannah and I wanted a bat mitzvah so badly our teeth hurt.

But Hannah is not me.

She is gutsier than I ever was or ever could hope to be, because at age twelve, Hannah does something I never would have done, which is to try to give herself a bat mitzvah—with or without anyone else's permission.

In order to do this book justice, I had to do a ton of research. I took Hebrew lessons, read dozens of Torah portions, interviewed rabbis, listened to podcasts, read Jewish stories, had more off-the-cuff conversations about God and Jewish identity and culture and tradition than I could count . . . and that's not including the dozens of batches of rugelach I made in order to accurately portray the kitchen scenes.

And I don't even like rugelach!

But the research pales in comparison to the amount of soul-searching I've done alongside it. By choosing to write a book about what it means to be Jewish, I'm implicitly claiming I'm Jewish enough to write it. And as someone who, like Hannah, has been told I'm not Jewish just as often as I'm told I am, I found myself struggling with granting myself the very permission my protagonist was searching for.

Sometimes I still feel like a fraud. But the good news is that this struggle is common. In fact, perhaps part of being Jewish is questioning what it means to be Jewish.

So even though I haven't reached any official conclusions about my own identity, I do know this: everyone, at one point or another, questions who they are. And this means none of us question alone.

To anyone who has ever felt the need to add an "ish" onto the end of their identity: you are not alone.

To anyone who has ever felt the way they celebrate their culture is wrong: you are not alone.

To anyone who sometimes feels like a marble swirl cake: you are not alone.

To anyone who feels the need to prove they are enough: you are not alone.

When it comes down to it, there is only one person in the entire world who can give you permission to be who you are.
And that person
is you.

Love,

Aimee Lucido

Acknowledgments

I have convinced myself the acknowledgments section of sophomore novels are supposed to be short. As if, now that I've been published once before, I no longer need to send screenshots of passages to my friends, beta readers, and family members in order to convince myself I am making good story choices.

Well, this is untrue, because publishing takes a village, but I do promise I will gush less this time around than I did in the acknowledgments section for my debut. I'm a professional now, goshdarnit.

First and foremost, thank you to my stalwart agent, Kathleen Rushall, who keeps me honest in all things publishing. To the incredible team at Versify—Margaret, Tara, Kwame—thank you for continuing to trust me to write books. When it comes down to it, that's all I want. Thank you to Emma Trihart and Celeste Knudsen for this gorgeous cover, and to Maxine Bartow and Mary Magrisso for being detail-oriented in a way I could never be.

To my friends and early readers—Lisa, Kate, Blair, Tasslyn, Ariel, Sofiya—your feedback and encouragement means the world to me. Thank you for continuing to let me send you screenshots of my edits and giving me both head pats and kicks in the pants when I need them.

To my expert readers, thank you for your honesty and forthrightness in your feedback. Any mistakes are my responsibility.

To my mom, who remains my first reader to this day: when you like the book, I know I've landed on something good. I trust your judgment to no end.

To anyone who discussed with me what it means to be Jewish—Lex, Rabbi Mates-Muchin, among others—you're the inspiration for this book. Thank you for your patience with me and my random "can I talk to you about Jewish ____" questions.

To Peter, I literally wouldn't be able to do this without you. Thank you for taking the leap with me.

To Bowser, you're the world's best dog.

And finally, to Ma and Pop. Thank you for giving me the permission to be Jewish I didn't realize I needed.

Praise and accolades for *Emmy in the Key of Code*

A Kids' Indie Next List Pick

Winner of the Nerdy Book Award

★ "As Emmy learns Java, the language and structure of programming seep into her poems. Music and code interweave. . . . And readers will cheer to see them work collectively . . . to create something beautiful."
— *Kirkus Reviews*, starred review

"Music, coding, strong female techie role models — this engaging first novel should attract a wide audience."
— *Booklist*

"This timely debut . . . champions girls in STEM and delivers a positive message about being 'always yourself.' . . . Through the author's creative mesh of coding, music, poetry, and narrative, this story uniquely conveys the art and beauty that can be found in multiple disciplines. . . . Relatable and relevant."
— *Publishers Weekly*

"This unusual tale seamlessly weaves basic computer coding concepts into a compelling story about middle schoolers struggling to forge their own identities in spite of the expectations of their families and society."
— *School Library Journal*

"*Emmy in the Key of Code* is a story about taking risks — about the risk of reaching out to a new friend, the risk of choosing a new place, the risk of forgiveness, and, most

especially, the risk of embracing a whole new way of imagining and expressing your life. It's thrilling to watch Emmy take these risks—and just as thrilling to watch Aimee Lucido ask her readers to do the same in this novel as innovative in its language as it is satisfying in its story."
—Gary Schmidt, Newbery Honor–winning author of
The Wednesday Wars

"In *Emmy in the Key of Code*, Aimee Lucido finds the poetry not just in computer coding, but in unexpected friendships, life-changing teachers, and that magical feeling of finding the place where you belong. A warm, wonderful book."
—Anne Ursu, author of *The Lost Girl*